A Willowdale, Indiana Story

I0555490

A Granddaughter's Promise

A Novel

Carla J. Underwood

Mud Pies Press
FOUNTAIN HILLS, ARIZONA

Copyright © 2018 by **Carla J. Underwood**

All rights reserved. No part of this publication may be reproduced, distributed or transmitted in any form or by any means, without prior written permission.

Carla J. Underwood/Mud Pies Press
13235 N. Verde River Dr., #308
Fountain Hills, Arizona 85268
www.mudpiespress.com
carla@mudpiespress.com

Publisher's Note: This is a work of fiction. Names, characters, places and incidents are a product of the author's imagination. Locales and public names are sometimes used for atmospheric purposes. Any resemblance to actual people, living or dead, or to businesses, companies, events, institutions, or locales is completely coincidental.

Cover Design © 2018 by Dawn Underwood
Book Layout © 2014 BookDesignTemplates.com
Cover Layout © 2014 BookDesignTemplates.com

A Granddaughter's Promise/Carla J. Underwood
1st edition
ISBN 978-0-9978780-4-2

Some people come into our lives and quickly go. Some stay for a while and leave footprints on our hearts, and we are never, ever the same.

—Author Unknown

Preface

Maude Ellis and Marie Ivey's lives were influenced by World Wars I and II and the Great Depression. Like other men and women of that era, they learned to be self-sufficient, to spend their money wisely and to share their hard-earned knowledge with future generations.

Because of the wisdom the two friends acquired during those difficult years, they were highly respected in their community. They became the touchstone by which the residents of Willowdale judged friendships and successful business practices.

When they chose to sell their businesses and retire, they remained true to the lessons they learned in life. To save money, they kept their pledge to one another to pool their funds and share a home. That decision influenced Shirley Ivey and the small town in ways Marie and Maude could never have predicted.

Table of Contents

One

"Ye gods, Shirley, stop the truck!"

When Grandma used that tone, I didn't ask questions. I slammed on the brakes.

I kept a tight grip on the stirring wheel, and she and Aunt Maude braced their hands against the dashboard. In a few seconds, Grandpa's old 1939 Chevrolet truck skidded to a stop.

"What's wrong, Grandma?"

I expected to see something blocking the street ahead, but there wasn't anything there. The only things on Main Street were three cars parked in front of the new Kut and Kurl beauty shop. All the other stores were still closed.

Aunt Maude dropped her hands from the dashboard and leaned forward. She looked past Grandma and out the passenger window.

"Would you look at that," she said.

"Now you see why we stopped, Maude," Grandma said. "The Elaine's sign is in its new location."

I pulled the truck into a diagonal parking space in front of Grandma's old café. While the engine idled, I rolled down the driver's window and rested my arm on the window frame.

"You wanted me to stop to see the sign?" I said. "I thought there was an emergency."

"It isn't an emergency," Grandma said, "but it illustrates how our little town changed while we were away."

"I suppose so," I said, "but the thing's still too big."

"It's all in the eyes of the beholder, young lady."

I was one beholder who hated the Elaine's sign, and not just because it was huge. It reminded me of Miss Carter's niece and all the trouble she caused our family.

"One thing's for sure," Aunt Maude said. "Nobody'll have trouble seeing it."

I had to laugh. Whoever moved the monstrous thing, attached it to the front section of the patio fence. It was the only space on the whole property big enough to hold it.

"There won't be any confusion it isn't my café any longer."

"That's true, Grandma," I said. "Let's just hope it doesn't knock the fence down."

I had to admit the purple lettering and the routed wildflowers around the border were pretty. As far as I was concerned, though, the size of it made it an eyesore.

"Let's not worry about the sign," Aunt Maude said. "I want to see our store."

"I'm with you," I said.

The store across the street from the café had been Aunt Maude's before she sold it to Miss Carter and moved to Illinois. Soon after she left, Grandma retired, sold the farmhouse and café and convinced her to move back home to Willowdale.

During the signing of the sales papers with Miss Carter, Grandma and Aunt Maude pooled their money and bought back Aunt Maude's old store. It was the perfect arrangement between two life-long friends.

They hired Jim Spencer to remodel it while we closed up the farmhouse and went to Illinois for Aunt Maude's things. Altogether, he had a month to finish the work.

The first thing they wanted him to do was turn the front of the store into a living area and library. The second thing was to divide the large apartment in the back into two smaller ones.

"Do you think Jim got the job done?" I said.

Grandma folded her hands in her lap and looked over at me. She grinned a little and nodded her head.

"Jimmy has had ample time to finish," she said.

"And he always keeps his word, Shirley."

I wanted to remind Aunt Maude how he broke his word and temporarily lost her pug, but I stopped myself. She treated him like a son, and Jim thought of her as a second mother after his own mother died. Anything I wanted to say would be hurtful, and I'd never do that to her.

"Let's go see your new home," I said.

Using the side view mirrors to guide me, I inched the truck backwards, straight across the street. I didn't stop until the rear tires touched the edge of the sidewalk in front of the store. I figured it would be easier to unload Aunt Maude's things that way.

"We're here," I said.

I turned off the engine and looked up and down Main Street searching for Mr. Spencer's truck. It's what Jim always drove, and he said he'd be there to help us.

"Where is he?" I said. "He should be here by now."

"Jim will be here," Aunt Maude said. "Just be patient."

After two weeks in Illinois packing her things, I was out of patience. I pushed the door open, eased out of the cab and turned to look at the store.

Neither Grandma nor Aunt Maude shared the finer details of the remodel with me. When I saw the changes Jim made to the front façade, my mouth dropped open.

"Wow."

I closed the driver's door, ran around the front of the truck and yanked the passenger door open. Grandma stepped from the cab, and Aunt Maude scooted across the seat. After she climbed out, the three of us stood side by side and studied the front of the store.

"It seems Jimmy followed our plans exactly, Maude."

"I don't know, Marie," she said. "It looks a lot fancier than I thought it would."

Instead of a simple canvas awning over the sidewalk like all the other stores, he built a shingled shed roof. It stretched the full width of the store, and its lower edge was supported by four wooden posts.

The screw holes on the gable where Miss Carter's sign once hung were patched. To hide the scars, Jim repainted the gable and the entire front of the store.

Under the front window, he built a long wooden bench. It looked identical to the one he built in front of the café.

My mind was racing, trying to take in the new look of the place. I wanted to tell Jim how fantastic it was, but I couldn't. I didn't know where he was.

"We can't wait for Jim all day," I said. "Let's go check out the place without him."

"That would be fine," Grandma said. "We did arrive a little earlier than expected."

She was right. I pushed on the gas pedal a little too hard and risked getting a speeding ticket to get back. I was anxious to see the remodel, but mostly, I wanted to see Jim.

I looked over at Grandma and Aunt Maude, and they grinned at me. I suspected they knew the main reason I had been in a hurry, and I felt my face turn red.

"We understand, dear," Grandma said. "I'm certain Jimmy will be along any minute."

"And you don't need to be embarrassed," Aunt Maude said.

What was I supposed to say? I liked Jim, but we had never been on an official date. I was relieved when Aunt Maude changed the subject.

"I used to hide a key on top of the door frame or under the doormat."

"I'll go check."

I jumped onto the sidewalk and raced to the front door. The key wasn't under the doormat, so I stood on my tiptoes and ran my hand along the top of the door frame.

"It's not here."

"See if it's taped to the trash barrel by the door."

I couldn't imagine anyone taping a key to a barrel, but I didn't question it. While she and Grandma watched, I felt all around the wooden barrel. I found the key near the bottom, secured by a strip of duct tape, and I ripped it off.

"Got it."

When I stood up, I noticed two familiar items attached to the front of the store. They made the outside remodel perfect.

To the left of the door, the wooden dowel from the old café was screwed to the wood siding. The four hooks were still on it and ready to hold Grandpa's American flag.

To the right of the door hung the "Beware, Guard Pug on Duty" sign Mr. Spencer made for Grandma. Since George was Willowdale's unofficial mascot, it was just the right greeting for anyone who knew the gentle, loveable pug.

"Good job, Jim," I said under my breath.

I didn't know what Miss Carter thought about the dowel and sign missing from her café, but I didn't care. They belonged to Grandma, and I was thrilled Jim thought to rescue them.

Grandma and Aunt Maude stood behind me without saying a word while I picked tape and glue from the key. When it was clean enough to use, I wadded up the tape, threw it into the barrel and slipped the key into the lock.

"This is it, Maude," Grandma said. "Our new home."

"Our new home, and your new library, Marie."

Before I turned the key, I looked back at them. They were smiling at me, but there were tears in their eyes. I couldn't blame them. Moving into their newly remodeled store was a whole new beginning.

"Here we go," I said.

When I turned the key and eased the door open, the smell of lavender and roses swept over me. I stood back and held the door while Grandma and Aunt Maude went inside.

"Ye gods and little fishes," Grandma said. "Look at this."

Just as I was about to follow them, something at the corner of my eye caught my attention. It was a glimpse of a little girl wearing a sundress.

I spun around to see who it was, but I wasn't fast enough. Before I saw her face, she ran across the sidewalk, jumped off the curb and ducked behind Grandpa's truck.

I was tempted to chase her and see what she was up to, but there was something more important to do. I put her out of my mind and went inside to see the rest of Jim's remodel.

TWO

Mr. Martin slammed the car door and stepped up onto the sidewalk in front of the café. He turned around and waved at Pastor Lawrence.

"Thanks fer the ride, Pastor," he said. "See ya later."

He plopped down on the bench in front of the window and watched the old sedan head out of town. The young pastor wouldn't be back to give him a ride home until the café closed at three o'clock.

"Gittin' old's not fer sissies," he said to himself.

He couldn't see to drive anymore, so he was grateful Miss Carter asked him to stay on as the café's handyman. She was too snooty for his tastes, but he needed the job to afford to stay in his little house.

"Not gonna live with that no-good brother of mine," he said. "No, sirree."

He pulled the old felt hat from his head, laid it on his lap and leaned against the bench's backrest. When he noticed Robert Ivey's old truck across the street, he took a deep breath and let out a loud sigh.

"Guess the ladies're back."

"Are you talkin' to me?"

He looked over his shoulder at the screen door and saw Irene, the café's cook, standing there. She wiped her hands on the front of her bib apron and smiled at him.

"Nope," he said. "Thinkin' out loud."

She opened the screen door and walked outside. Her blond hair hung in a single braid down her back and wagged back and forth as she walked.

When she got closer, he saw smeared bacon grease all over the front of her apron. Her plump cheeks were red, and dots of perspiration lined her upper lip.

"Cookin' already?" he said.

"Have to be ready for when Miss Carter shows up."

"Yep," he said. "'Bout time ta open."

She sat down on the opposite end of the bench and straightened her skirt over her knees. With the hem of her apron, she wiped the perspiration from her face and looked across the street.

"Seen them yet?" she said.

He reached into his pants pocket and pulled out a rumpled hankie. While he rotated his hat in an endless circle, he wiped the inside of the hatband.

"Nope," he said. "Just lookin' at Robert's truck."

Its bed was heaped with boxes and a double-sized mattress and box spring. Wooden-spindled head and foot boards were tucked along the sides, and the entire load was lashed down with a frayed rope.

"Hope they like what Jimmy did," Irene said.

"I'm thinkin' they like it just fine."

18

"Marie's about as picky as they come, you know."

"Yep," he said. "I surely do."

He had worked for her in the old café long enough to know she liked things to be perfect. When he moved her boxes and furniture from the farmhouse, he made sure they were put in their proper places in the store.

There was one more thing he knew for sure. She was the boss during the remodel, and his friendship with her late husband didn't count for anything. If he wanted to get paid for the work he did while she was in Illinois, things better be done right.

Three

"Wow."

That was all I could manage to say. Jim's remodel on the inside looked amazing.

Grandma and Aunt Maude seemed to be as dumbfounded as I was and didn't say anything. All of us stood near the front door and stared at all the changes he made.

Instead of only the three original floor-to-ceiling bookcases, Jim built another one. All four jutted into the room, perpendicular to the front door, with narrow aisles separating them. On the end of each bookcase was a sign with a range of letters written on it. I didn't know how Jim organized the books, but every shelf was at least half-full.

In front of the bookcases, the two overstuffed sofas and coffee table Miss Carter sold with the store were grouped together. There was a built-in seat under the front window, and framed photos of the original general store hung along the side wall.

On the opposite side of the room, Jim hung a replica of the store's original mailbox cabinet on the wall. Some slots contained letters or small packages, and a narrow counter, similar to the original, stood beneath the cabinet.

Around the perimeter of the room, he covered the bottom half of the walls with wainscoting made of bead board. The wood was painted a deep shade of grey, and the walls above it were painted off-white.

He created a simple coffered ceiling that extended over the entire space. The wooden squares were painted the same dark grey as the wainscoting. A frosted globe light hung from the center of each square and above each aisle between the bookcases.

"Ye gods and little fishes."

"Oh, my."

Aunt Maude put her hand over her heart and slowly turned in place. She stopped when she saw what was near the front door.

"Look, Marie."

Against the windowless wall facing the street, Jim installed a potbellied stove with a glass window in its door. The wall behind the stove and the floor underneath it were covered in various-sized pieces of slate.

"Just like in your café's storeroom, Grandma."

A brocade armchair stood on either side of the stove, and in front of each was a small wooden footstool. Grandma's favorite afghan was draped over the arm of the chair on the left. The blanket Aunt Maude's pug loved was on the floor next to the chair on the right.

"That young man thought of every detail," Grandma said.

Aunt Maude was smiling, but her face looked pale. I wondered if all the changes were too much for her weak heart.

"I need to take a breather," she said.

She walked over to the potbellied stove and sank into the chair next to George's blanket. When she put her feet up on the stool, she let out a deep sigh.

"That's better."

Grandma turned toward the back of the room and walked the full length of the closest bookcase. As she went, she trailed her hand along the spines of the books.

"Beautiful," she said. "Just beautiful."

While Aunt Maude rested and Grandma admired the books, I inspected the rest of the main room. The area beyond the mailboxes and the small counter was divided into two spaces.

One space was an L-shaped kitchen open to the rest of the room. Grandma's kitchen table and chairs stood in the center of the space, and a globe light hung over the table. A smaller light hung above the sink.

The space beyond the kitchen was enclosed. Its door faced the bookcases, and when I opened it I discovered an enormous pantry. Every wall held six shelves, and half of them were filled with Grandma's dishes, pots and pans and precious keepsakes.

"Wow."

I stood in the center of the pantry and marveled at how much storage Jim had incorporated into his design. His passion for architecture was on display in every detail of the remodel.

While I studied the shelves, Grandma came inside and stood next to me. She crossed her arms in front of her chest and nodded.

"What do you think, dear?"

"I think it's wonderful."

"It is, isn't it?"

She uncrossed her arms and walked back into the main room. I turned and followed right behind her like a little puppy.

"Shirley and I are anxious to see the rest of the rooms," she said. "How about you, Maude?"

Aunt Maude eased out of her chair and joined us at an arched doorway in the center of the back wall. Its purpose was obvious to me. It provided separation between the main room and the private areas at the back of the store.

"My apartment should be over here."

Aunt Maude led Grandma and me down a short hallway to our left. A door at the end of the hall stood wide open, and the scent of lavender grew stronger.

We walked in and stood in the center of the empty room. Two sash windows on the back wall had no curtains or blinds, and the space was bathed in sunlight.

"Once my furniture is in here, it won't look so big."

Maybe not, I thought to myself, but it was still a big room. There was plenty of space for her double bed, her dresser and her desk and chair.

"It's going to be perfect, Aunt Maude."

On the other side of the room was a small bathroom, and next to it was a sitting nook. Her easy chair, her television console and George's things would easily fit there.

The lavender smell grew even stronger the farther we walked toward that side of the room. It was so strong, I wanted to pinch my nose shut, but I didn't. I knew it was Aunt Maude's favorite scent.

"Over here, Shirley."

Aunt Maude took my wrist and pulled me toward the bathroom. She reached inside the door and plucked one of several sachets from a ceramic bowl on the edge of the sink.

"Here," she said. "It's a housewarming gift for you."

The small net bag was filled with dried lavender and pulled closed at the top with a narrow pink ribbon. I thought it was sweet of her to share it with me, but I was confused.

"Aunt Maude," I said. "This is your new home, not mine."

"It is?"

What was that supposed to mean? Didn't she feel at home?

Before I could ask her, Grandma clapped her hands and hurried to the bedroom door. She grinned at me, and her eyes sparkled.

"Now, it's my turn," she said.

Aunt Maude and I followed her to the opposite end of the hallway. On the way, we passed a closed door, but neither of them mentioned it. I imagined it was only the furnace room, so I didn't say anything either.

"Here it is," Grandma said.

Her apartment was the same size and configuration as Aunt Maude's but with a reversed footprint. It seemed smaller because it was filled with her bedroom furniture from the farmhouse.

The bathroom was identical to Aunt Maude's, too, but Grandma's sitting nook was already furnished. Grandpa's leather chair, his footstool and the cabinet holding his Philco radio took up most of the space. Just enough room was left beside the chair for the wicker basket filled with the rest of Grandma's crocheted afghans. Stacked beside the radio were more of her books and our family Bible.

"This is perfect for you, Grandma."

"Jimmy has done himself proud," Aunt Maude said.

On the nightstand beside the bed was a bouquet of white and yellow roses. They were beautifully arranged in the old porcelain vase with the gaudy red roses painted on it.

"Well, now," Grandma said. "How did Jimmy know this is my favorite vase?"

"I don't know," I said. "Where did he get the roses?"

Both Grandma and Aunt Maude turned toward me. They smiled and shook their heads.

"Shirley," Aunt Maude said. "Anybody can see they came from your Grandma's old rose garden."

"Yikes," I said. "What will Miss Carter say about that?"

"I assume," Grandma said, "she won't object to me enjoying one final bouquet."

Four

Once Shirley went inside the store, Cindy Thomas abandoned her hiding place behind the truck and raced across the street. She crouched inside the café's patio area and watched the store through a gap in the fence boards below the huge sign.

Only seconds after she hid there, Mr. Martin arrived and Irene came out of the café. They sat on the bench and talked and talked. She couldn't make out what they said, but she was afraid they would never stop.

She finally got tired of crouching and sat down on the limestone pavers. Her thin sundress was no protection against the cold stone, and her right calf developed a cramp.

"Ouch," she whispered.

She tried to ignore the pain, but it was impossible. The muscle was in a tight knot.

Standing up would have eased the pain, but she didn't want anyone to see her hiding. She stretched out her leg and massaged the knot with her thumbs.

When Mr. Martin and Irene didn't get up and leave after a few more minutes, she got tired of waiting. She decided to make her move.

She turned onto her hands and knees and crawled across the patio. The pavers were rough against her bare knees, but she didn't make a sound.

At the gate in the back section of the fence, she stood up and took several deep breaths. She brushed out the wrinkles in her sundress, rubbed dirt from her sore knees and eased the gate open.

She scanned the empty lot beyond the fence and waited a second or two. When she didn't see anyone, she darted out of the gate and ran as fast as she could across the lot.

When she reached the edge of the graveled alley, she stopped and gasped for a full breath of air. Dr. Thompson warned her running was bad for her heart, but she didn't have a choice. She didn't want to get caught sneaking around.

"I just wanted to see what the store looks like," she said to herself.

Every day for two weeks, she had stood in the beauty shop's window and watched Jim Spencer and the other workers. They went in and out of the store all day long with tools and supplies.

She ached to go in and see the construction, but she was too new to the small town. There was no one she knew well enough to ask.

"Maybe I can ask Shirley to show me."

She wished she had the nerve to go back to the store and ask for a tour, but they just got back to town. She thought the last thing Shirley needed was a little girl bothering her.

Besides that, her mother was waiting for her at the shop, and she had been gone too long already. Asking to see the remodel would have to wait until later.

She took a few more deep breaths and ran down the alley toward the beauty shop. She kicked up her heels and pumped her arms. With each step, her braids whipped back and forth against her back.

"I'm coming, Mama."

By the time she reached the shop's back door, her lungs hurt and her windpipe burned. Instead of stopping to rest, she pulled the door open and walked inside.

Her mother was at the front of the shop, standing behind a customer and pulling curlers out of the woman's hair. Two other women sat under dryer hoods along the far wall. Neither of them bothered to look up from their magazines and say hello to her.

She ignored them, walked up to the woman in the swivel chair and looked at her mother's reflection in the wall mirror. Her mother looked back at her without turning around.

"There you are," she said. "I was getting worried."

"I'm sorry, Mama."

She remembered exactly when her mother had begun to worry about her. It was right after her last birthday, and the doctor diagnosed her with an irregular heartbeat.

A few days later, her father moved away from the farm without saying goodbye and left her mother with all the bills. They had to move to Willowdale so she could go to work in the beauty shop.

"Why didn't Papa come with us?"

"Because it's just the two of us now," her mother had said. "Someday you'll understand."

She continued to stare at her mother's reflection while she worked on the woman's hair. For the first time, she noticed the furrows in her forehead and the deep lines at the corners of her mouth. She couldn't remember the last time she heard her mother laugh.

"I'm really sorry I'm late, Mama," she said.

"Where have you been?"

Her mother spun the customer's chair away from the mirror and pulled out more curlers. The lady's grey hair had a hint of blue.

"I went to the end of Main Street and back," she said.

"Main Street must have gotten longer since you left."

"I walked real slow."

When her mother looked down at her and frowned, she knew she wasn't fooling her. She was still out of breath.

"Next time you go for a walk, don't run."

"Yes, Mama."

She stood and watched while her mother brushed out the woman's hair. She hoped the blueish color looked better without curlers, but it didn't.

"Mama," she said. "I know what I want to be when I grow up."

"I hope it isn't to be a hairdresser."

"Oh, Mama," she said. "I want to be a hero."

"What made you think of that?"

"I don't know."

"Cindy?"

"Okay," she said. "I want to be a hero just like Shirley."

Her mother stopped brushing the woman's hair. She turned around and rested her free hand on her hip.

"I'm thankful Shirley rescued you during the storm at the lake last summer," she said, "but nobody expects you to be like her."

"But, Mama,—"

"That's enough," she said. "You need to go rest now."

"Do I have to?"

Her mother shook her head and frowned again. She probably wasn't angry, but the woman with the blue hair didn't sound happy.

"Go take your nap," the woman said. "Your mother's busy."

She dropped her chin, turned around and walked toward the back of the shop. She hated the army cot in the backroom, and she hated taking naps. After all, she was nine years old, not a baby.

"I am, too, going to be a hero someday, Mama," she said under her breath. "Just wait and see."

In the backroom, she kicked off her shoes, sprawled on the cot and covered herself with a blanket. She reached over to the side table and picked up her favorite comic book. Within minutes, she fell asleep while reading the superhero's latest adventure.

Five

I left Grandma and Aunt Maude in Grandma's apartment and wandered back into the main room. I didn't know what to do with the sachet, so I stuffed it in the back pocket of my jeans.

The remodel was beautiful, but where did that leave me? There were still two weeks left before I was to go back home, and I didn't have a bed to sleep in.

"Come on, Shirley," I said to myself. "You can think of something."

I walked over to the sitting area and studied the two overstuffed sofas. The one nearest the bookcases looked comfortable, and it gave me a clear view of Main Street.

I decided I could sleep there well enough, and I wouldn't be in anybody's way. There was even room in the pantry to store my blanket and pillow during the day.

"That'll work."

Even though I solved the sleeping situation, my lower lip slipped into its old pout. I thought I'd outgrown that habit, and I felt disgusted. It was a special day for Grandma and Aunt Maude, and all I did was feel sorry for myself.

"Stop it," I said. "This is their new home, not yours."

"Shirley, dear?"

I spun around when I heard Grandma's voice and tucked my bottom lip back into place. She and Aunt Maude were standing in the arched doorway, smiling at me.

"What is it, Grandma?"

"Are you ready to see the rest of the remodel?"

"There's more?"

"Oh, my, yes," Aunt Maude said.

I couldn't imagine what else there could be. The only possible room left to see was behind the door in the hallway. It had to be a boring utility room, but I wanted to humor them.

"Lead on," I said and giggled a little too loudly.

When I walked over to them, Grandma swung open the mysterious door, and I stood in disbelief. Just when I thought Jim couldn't pull off one more surprise, he did.

Behind the door was a circular staircase winding upward toward the attic. Beyond the staircase was a wide hallway leading to a half-glass back door.

Along one wall stood a clothes washer and dryer, a utility sink, a furnace and a water heater. Along the opposite wall were several storage cabinets.

"Jim really did think of everything, Grandma."

"Oh, there's more," she said.

"Go on," Aunt Maude said. "See where those stairs go."

"What?"

"Up you go," she said. "We'll be right behind you."

My curiosity got the better of me, and I sprinted up the stairs without waiting for them. At the top was a small landing with two closed doors. One faced the front of the store, the other faced the back.

"Which one do I open first?"

"You pick," Aunt Maude called from the bottom of the stairs.

I debated with myself for only a second and decided to open the door facing the front. Inside was a storeroom half-filled with boxes from the farmhouse, old furniture and a foot-locker I'd never seen before.

The lid on the locker was open, and several books were stacked in the top tray. Grandma probably wanted them downstairs, so I picked them up, closed the lid and stacked them on top of the locker. I'd go back later to get them.

The light in the room came from a small gable window facing Main Street. When I looked outside, the water tower behind Grandma's old café looked all cheery with its bright red lettering.

"Hi, old friend," I said.

Grandma and Aunt Maude were nearly halfway up the staircase, but I still didn't wait for them. I closed the store-room door and opened the one facing the back.

When I saw what was inside, I stopped short. My mouth dropped open and my eyes filled with tears.

Grandma and Aunt Maude finally reached the landing and stood on either side of me. Grandma put her hand on my arm.

"Well, dear," she said. "What do you think?"

I thought I was dreaming, but I knew I was wide awake. In front of me was a nearly perfect replica of my tiny bedroom at the farmhouse.

It didn't have a dormer window, but Jim did the next best thing. He constructed a built-in seat under the small gable window and arranged all of my furniture the way it used to be. Even the same spread was on the bed, and the same afghan was folded across the foot.

"Wow," I said. "Oh, wow."

"Does that mean you like it?" Aunt Maude said.

I threw an arm around both of them, pulled them to me and gave them both a hug. I didn't just like the room. I loved it.

"Aunt Maude," I said. "You told me somebody at the auction spoke for all of my furniture."

"Somebody did," she said. "Me."

I let go of them, and tears streamed down my cheeks. I brushed them away with the palms of my hands, and wiped my hands on my jeans.

"I thought I was going to sleep on a sofa," I said and sniffed back more tears.

"Ye gods, young lady, stop your crying," Grandma said. "We have a truck to unload."

"Yes, Grandma."

"By the way," she said. "I hope you don't mind we had Jimmy add two new items to your room."

"You did?"

We turned around, and I saw the rest of the bedroom for the first time. To the left of the door was a long, narrow walk-in closet tucked up under the eave. To the right of the door was a bathroom squeezed into a larger space under the opposite eave.

"Oh, wow."

My mouth dropped open again. How could I mind a bathroom and closet of my very own? I was in heaven.

"We decided it's about time you have some privacy," Aunt Maude said.

I walked across the room, pulled the sachet from my pocket and laid it on top of my dresser. I finally understood what Aunt Maude meant. It truly was a housewarming gift for me.

"I love everything," I said. "Thank you."

"Remember, dear," Grandma said. "As long as Maude or I live here, you will always have a home in Willowdale."

Six

Mr. Martin sat at the lunch counter and watched Irene through the kitchen service window. The sight of her cooking gave him some comfort, but it wasn't the same. Without Mrs. Ivey and her granddaughter there, the café felt cold and lifeless.

When he heard a knock on the door, he spun on the stool and looked out the front window. Clyde Wilson was standing at the door, but his parked truck was still idling. After a few seconds, the engine finally died.

"Clyde's here," he said to Irene.

Without waiting for the young man to knock again, he stood up, went to the door and unlocked it. When he pulled the door open, Clyde nodded at him.

"Morning, Mr. Martin."

"Mornin', Clyde," he said. "Yer here kinda early."

"I need coffee before I drive over to Monticello."

It was too early to open, but he stood back and let Clyde in anyway. He figured the boy needed coffee alright, but that wasn't the only reason he was there.

"Morning, Irene," Clyde said and hurried toward the far end of the lunch counter.

When Irene saw him, she smiled and grabbed the coffeepot from the stove. She carried it into the dining room with one hand and two coffee mugs by their handles with the other.

"Sit down, you two," she said. "Coffee's ready."

He did as she said and sat on the stool near the door. Clyde sat on the stool near the service window, and Irene stopped in front of him. The two grinned at each other.

She set the mugs on the counter and filled both of them with steaming coffee. One of them she slid down the counter, and he stopped it before it toppled off the end. She handed the other mug to Clyde, set the coffeepot on the counter and stared at him.

"Hi," she said.

When they grinned at each other again, he picked up his mug and turned away to give them some privacy. He was about to take a sip of the coffee, but he stopped when he heard the back door slam shut.

"Uh-oh," he said.

He put the mug down and watched Miss Carter rush into the dining room with a bundle of newspapers in her arms. She passed by the counter and dropped the bundle on the floor in front of the magazine rack.

"You would think that boy had enough sense to arrange for a substitute while he's away," she said.

"Ya mean Jimmy?"

"Of course, I mean Jim, Mr. Martin," she said. "Who else?"

He laughed to himself when Irene snatched the coffeepot off the counter and hurried back to the kitchen. Clyde stayed right where he was, drank his coffee without looking up and didn't say a word.

Miss Carter continued to stand next to the bundle of newspapers and stare at them. He didn't know what she expected him to do about the situation.

"What's the matter with Jimmy?" he said.

She turned around, jammed her fists on her hips and glared at him. Seeing her angry so early in the morning made him suspect the rest of his day might be a challenge.

"He abandoned his duties," she said. "I had to retrieve these papers from in front of the bank myself."

He was tempted to smile at her childish outburst, but that would only make her madder. He couldn't afford to get himself fired his first day on the job.

"Ya want me ta git 'em tomorrow?"

"That would be acceptable," she said. "I'll call the newspaper office and request a replacement for Jim."

"He's comin' back in a couple days, ya know."

She didn't say any more about the newspapers and scanned the empty dining room. When she saw Clyde at the counter, she ignored him, turned toward the front window and looked outside.

"Where are all my customers, Mr. Martin?"

"Couldn't say fer sure."

"Shouldn't there be a line of people waiting to come inside?"

It was obvious no one was waiting, so he didn't know what she wanted him to say. He only knew he no longer had an appetite for coffee.

He left the untouched mug on the counter and wandered over to the bundle on the floor. While Miss Carter watched, he untied the twine that held the papers together.

"Don't ya worry none," he said.

"What do you mean by that?"

He took off his old hat, hung it on a hook by the front door and snatched an old newspaper from the rack. He tossed it on the floor and replaced it with a new one from the bundle.

"I like deliverin' papers," he said. "Used ta have my own route, ya know."

"Very well, I won't make that call to the newspaper," she said. "You are more than welcome to pick up the café's papers until Jim returns."

Seven

I untied the rope from the top of the load, coiled it up and tossed it inside the cab. Then, I stepped back a few feet to get a good look at everything in the back of the truck.

If I had to, I knew I could unload the boxes by myself. My arm muscles were strong from moving around boxes at the farmhouse and at Aunt Maude's brother's place in Illinois.

The heavy, bulky furniture was a different story. I couldn't unload them alone, and I couldn't expect Grandma and Aunt Maude to help at their age.

While I tried to think of a solution to my problem, I heard the constant beep of a horn. I walked back to the cab, slammed the door shut and looked in the direction of the sound.

"Jim?"

West of town, Mr. Spencer's truck bumped along the gravel road, raising a cloud of dust. The closer it came, I saw Mr. Spencer behind the wheel, not Jim.

George was standing on the other side of the seat with his head poking out the passenger window. His tongue hung out of his mouth, and his little ears flapped in the wind.

When I waved at them, the honking stopped, and George sat down. I could barely see the top of his head.

Mr. Spencer drove onto Main Street's pavement, did a U-turn and eased his truck into the parking space beside me. Before I could say anything, George stood up again and wagged at me.

"Hi, George," I said. "Hi, Mr. Spencer."

"Good morning, Shirley," he said. "Welcome back."

I leaned into the passenger window and scratched behind the little pug's ears. I tried to give him a kiss on the top of his wrinkled head, but he licked my nose instead.

"Oh, George," I said. "I sure have missed you."

I backed myself out of the window, opened the door and picked him up. He seemed a little plump around the middle.

"Where's Jim?" I said. "He told me he'd help unload the truck."

"He's in Lafayette for a couple of days."

"Lafayette?"

Mr. Spencer turned off the truck's engine and stepped out of the cab. He walked around to the back of Grandpa's truck and eyed Aunt Maude's things.

"A friend drove him over there for an interview," he said.

"He never told me anything about an interview."

I didn't know why I said that, and I immediately regretted it. Jim and I weren't an official couple, and he didn't owe me any explanation.

Before Mr. Spencer said anything more, Aunt Maude rushed outside and stood on the edge of the sidewalk. When George saw her, he wagged so hard I could barely hang onto him.

"Okay, okay, big guy."

I walked between the trucks and set George on the sidewalk beside her. Without a backward glance, he bumped headfirst into her leg and wagged until his whole body wiggled.

"There's my boy," she said. "Did you behave yourself for Bill?"

"He was the perfect guest, Aunt Maude."

"Thanks for watching him for me."

"Glad to do it."

George followed at her heel when she walked to the front door, and they went into the store together. The last thing I saw before the door closed was George's curly tail wagging at top speed.

"Well, Shirley," Mr. Spencer said. "Let's get this stuff unloaded."

He stood on the sidewalk behind the tailgate of Grandpa's truck, and I climbed into the bed. Every box was marked where it should go inside the store, and I handed them to him one at a time.

He divided the boxes into three stacks along the sidewalk. One stack was for the pantry, one was for Aunt Maude's apartment and one was for the attic storeroom. When we finished, the only things left to unload were Aunt Maude's bedroom and sitting nook furniture.

I jumped down from the truck and studied the three piles of boxes. My back started to ache. I'd forgotten how many boxes we brought from Illinois.

"It's official," Mr. Spencer said. "I need a rest."

"That sounds good to me, too."

He sat on one end of the bench and rubbed his lower back with his hands. I sat on the other end of the bench and watched him. It was amazing how someone his age had as much stamina as he did.

"Too bad Jim couldn't be here to help," I said. "What kind of interview is it?"

"It's for an internship."

"An internship?"

"With a fancy architect firm."

I was disappointed Jim wasn't there to help, but I understood how important the interview was. Being offered an internship was a huge compliment.

"Andy told his father about my Jimmy."

"I don't know who Andy is."

"He's in the same class as Jimmy," he said. "It's his father's architect business."

I nodded. Jim was smart, and he worked hard on all of his remodeling projects. He deserved recognition.

"Jim's only going to be a senior in high school," I said. "How can he get an internship?"

"Mr. Andersen really liked the work he did here and over at the café."

He stopped rubbing his back and leaned against the backrest. He drew in a deep breath and let it out with a long, heavy sigh.

"He wants my boy to work in his office on weekends during school."

"Wow."

"Next summer, he wants him to work full-time."

That was impressive by anyone's standard, but I worried about Mr. Spencer. I always assumed Jim would help his dad at the mill until he left for Purdue.

"What're you going to do without his help?"

Mr. Spencer didn't answer. He closed his eyes and folded his hands on his lap. The knuckles were red and swollen, and I couldn't imagine how painful they were.

"You stay here and rest," I said. "I'll be right back."

I stood up and looked up and down Main Street. The same three cars were parked in front of the new beauty shop, and Clyde's truck was parked in front of the café.

Without hesitating, I jumped off the sidewalk, raced across the street and stopped at the café's front door. I heard Miss Carter and Mr. Martin talking, and I paused a moment with my hand on the door handle.

I didn't want to deal with Miss Carter after the trouble her niece caused me, but I didn't have a choice. Mr. Spencer and I desperately needed Clyde's help.

As I pulled the screen door open, I saw the faded bricks where Grandpa's wooden dowel used to be attached. Knowing Jim had the nerve to remove it for Grandma gave me the boost of courage I needed. I lifted my chin, forced a smile and walked into the café to face Miss Carter.

Eight

Elaine sat at the front table of her café, watched the action across the street and scowled. Shirley and Clyde were unloading furniture from the old truck, and Mr. Spencer was sitting on the bench, watching them.

"That girl certainly had a lot of nerve," she said to herself, "coming here and taking away my only customer."

She didn't like Shirley's method, but if Clyde wanted to volunteer to help, there wasn't anything she could do. Besides, he was only one customer and never bought anything but coffee anyway. She was certain a paying customer would arrive any moment.

It was when Mr. Martin volunteered to help, she put her foot down. A cheapskate customer like Clyde was one thing. An employee was something entirely different.

"What kind of an employer would I be if I were to allow my employees to do whatever they like?"

After she denied Mr. Martin's request to leave, he and Irene stopped speaking to her. They made their feelings known in their own special ways.

In the kitchen, Irene stirred the pots and pans on the stove with huge metal spoons. She let the sink faucet run at maximum capacity and turned the vent fan to its highest speed.

In the old storeroom, Mr. Martin unloaded boxes and filled display cases for the new gift shop. Every time he emptied a cardboard box, he grumbled and tossed it into the hall several feet away. Each one landed with a loud thud.

She knew all the noise was meant to annoy, but she wouldn't allow them to intimidate her. She was their boss, not their friend. They needed to understand that distinction right from the start.

"I can't worry about their hurt feelings," she said under her breath. "I have more important concerns."

The biggest concern was luring customers to her café. It was a challenge competing with Willowdale's decades-old devotion to the Ivey family.

"I simply must discover my own niche in this community."

She knew dwelling on the issue was a waste of energy. She needed to take action.

The phone on the wall next to the service window was already transferred to her name. She got up, walked over to it and picked up the receiver. The operator came on the line immediately.

"Marie?"

"This is Elaine Carter, Harriet," she said.

"I'm so sorry, Miss Carter."

"I'm willing to overlook your mistake this time," she said, "but I don't expect it to become a habit."

"Of course not, Miss Carter," Harriet said. "What can I do for you?"

"I would like to speak with the editor of the Monticello newspaper."

There was a long pause, and Elaine wondered if the operator disconnected the call. She was about to hang up when Harriet came back on again.

"Thank you for waiting, Miss Carter," she said. "The editor is on the line."

Elaine waited until she heard a click and was certain the operator wasn't listening. Her business was none of that nosy woman's concern.

"Hello," she said. "This is Elaine Carter calling from Willowdale."

"I'm Howard Drake," he said. "What can I do for you, Miss Carter?"

"Well, Mr. Drake, I'm the owner of Elaine's.

"What's Elaine's?"

She winced at the slight, but the man's lack of knowledge spoke volumes. She forced herself to remain calm and speak civilly to him.

"Elaine's is the new name of Mrs. Ivey's café," she said. "I'm the new owner."

"I see," he said. "What's this all about?"

For several minutes, she outlined the advertising campaign she conceived. When he didn't laugh at her idea for drawing customers to her café, she made a mental note. The man seemed intelligent, and he was more accepting of her innovative idea than she had feared he would be.

"Let me get this straight," he said. "You want to print coupons in the advertising section and with your announcement in the business section."

"That's correct, Mr. Drake," she said. "The coupons must be large enough for customers to clip and bring to the café."

"I see."

She heard scratching noises and imagined him writing down her demands. Then, the man cleared his throat.

"What else was it you wanted?"

"I want a reporter to interview me," she said. "A story to fill the top fold of the front page seems appropriate."

There was a long pause. She understood the man needed to consider such a request, but she felt her story was front page worthy.

"There's just one thing," he said. "If the article runs on the front page instead of with the local news, it'll cost you extra."

"I never doubted that," she said. "Your best reporter and the top fold of the front page, agreed?"

"I'll send out the reporter next week."

"Tomorrow, Mr. Drake, and you'll run the article in the Sunday edition."

There was another long pause. She didn't know what he would charge her for her demands. It wouldn't be inexpensive, but she would pay whatever it took for the publicity.

"Do we understand each other, Mr. Drake?"

"We do, Miss Carter," he said. "The reporter will see you tomorrow, and he'll have your bill with him."

Nine

"I'll be right back, Mama," Cindy said. "I'll try not to run."

"Don't go too far," her mother said. "I'll close up shop in a little while."

She napped longer than she had planned and needed to hurry if she wanted to see the remodel. Rubbing the sleep from her eyes, she waved goodbye to her mother and rushed out the front door.

She stopped at the curb and looked at the old truck up the street. It was still parked in front of Mrs. Ivey's store, but the back of it was empty.

"Oh, no," she said.

She ran across the street and walked up the sidewalk in the direction of the store. About half-way there the door opened, and Shirley walked out with two bulging gunny sacks in her hands. To keep from being seen, she ducked behind the nearest trash barrel and waited.

After Shirley tossed the sacks into the truck bed and went back inside, she stood up again. She crept along the inside edge of the sidewalk and stopped at the store with her back pressed against the wall.

She took a deep breath, turned toward the front window and pressed her nose and her cupped hands against the glass. Even with her hands shielding her eyes, it was hard to see through the dirty window.

Everyone in the store looked a little distorted, but she recognized everybody. Shirley stood in the center of the room with her back to the window. Mrs. Ivey and Aunt Maude sat on a sofa with their feet on a coffee table in front of them.

She watched and listened for several seconds. She wanted to knock on the door when she knew the moment was right, but their voices were too muffled to understand. To help her hear better, she leaned one ear closer to the glass.

"That should be the last of the trash for now," Mrs. Ivey said.

"I'm tired," Aunt Maude said. "Let's call it a day."

"I'll go move the truck, Grandma."

When Shirley turned around and walked toward the door, she ducked down. The bench under the window was too narrow to completely conceal her, but there was nowhere else to hide. She sat beside it, tucked her legs close to her chest and wrapped her arms around her knees.

She wanted to see the store more than anything, but she didn't want to bother them when they were tired. She decided she could wait one more day.

Shirley walked outside, climbed into the cab of the truck and started the engine. With one eye closed, she watched the old truck turn around and park diagonally in front of the store.

When she heard the truck door slam shut and Shirley's footsteps on the sidewalk, she closed both eyes. She didn't open them again until she heard the front door open and close.

Without a watch, she wasn't sure what time it was, but she knew her mother wanted to close the shop. Staying out of sight, she duck-walked to the corner of the store, jumped up and ran down the sidewalk toward Kut and Kurl.

Ten

Sarah Thomas combed her final customer's hair and stood back to see the result. It was a short cut and didn't require special care. She almost regretted charging the woman for it.

"Very nice," the woman said.

While her customer admired her reflection in the mirror, she walked to the front window. She hadn't seen her daughter for nearly half an hour.

"Where are you, Cindy?"

When she turned around, the woman stepped down from the chair and picked up her purse. She pulled out the money she owed and handed it to her.

"You know," the woman said. "Sometimes my youngest granddaughter spends the day at Mrs. Van Berkel's."

"Mrs. Van Berkel?"

"She lives on a farm east of town and does babysitting for children your daughter's age."

"I can't afford something like that."

The woman snapped her purse closed and laid a twenty-five-cent tip on the counter in front of the chair. She walked to the front door but stopped before going outside.

"Mrs. Van Berkel is very nice," she said, "and she's good with kids."

What she earned as a hairdresser barely paid the bills, but the woman had a point. It wasn't good for Cindy to wander around all day by herself.

"I'll think about it," she said.

When the woman walked outside, she walked out with her and looked up and down the street for Cindy. She saw her across the street, running at top speed down the sidewalk.

"Cindy," she said. "Slow down."

Her daughter stopped only long enough for a truck to pass. Then, she ran across the street, plopped down on the bench in front of the shop and gasped for air. Her sundress was wrinkled, and her face was smudged with dirt.

"Oh, Cindy," she said. "What have you been up to?"

She sat down next to her daughter and wrapped an arm around her shoulders. She pulled her close and waited.

When Cindy's chest quit heaving, she lifted her arm off her shoulders. She turned toward her daughter and studied her face.

"I was worried, Cindy."

"I know, Mama, but I got back here as soon as I could."

She didn't know what that meant, and she didn't have the energy to ask. She knew her daughter spent too much time unsupervised, but what was a broke, divorced mother to do?

"Go wash up, sweetie," she said. "It's time to lock up."

"Yes, Mama."

Eleven

Mr. Martin waved goodbye to Pastor Lawrence and went inside his little house. He hung his hat on the coat rack, unfastened the key chain from his belt and looped it over a hook by the door.

Dishes from the last two days were stacked in the sink, but he was too tired to wash them. Instead, he shuffled into the living room and over to his recliner.

"My back's killin' me," he said to himself. "I never wanna see another box."

He eased himself into the chair and kicked off his shoes. On the table beside him was a half-filled glass of iced tea from the night before.

The liquid was cloudy, and there was dark residue on the bottom of the glass. It didn't look a bit appetizing to him, but he was thirsty. He picked up the glass, stared at it for only a second and gulped down every drop.

"There," he said to the glass. "Ya don't need washin' now."

He set the glass on the table and reached for the lever on the side of the chair. Before he had a chance to raise the footrest, the telephone rang. For several seconds, he stared at the wall phone in the kitchen and debated ignoring it.

"Who'd be callin' me anyways?"

After the fifth ring, he couldn't stand listening to the noise any longer. He pushed himself up from the chair and shuffled into the kitchen. On the tenth ring, he picked up the receiver.

"Yeah, Harriet," he said. "What's goin' on?"

"Thank goodness you're home," she said. "Mrs. Ivey's calling."

Once the café opened for the day, he became Miss Carter's handyman, not Mrs. Ivey's. There was no reason for her to call. Having one demanding boss at a time was all he could handle.

"What's she want?"

"She didn't say, but she's been trying to reach you ever since the café closed."

His back hurt, he was dead tired, and he wasn't in the mood to talk to Mrs. Ivey. Every time she called it meant only one thing. She needed him to do something for her.

"Okay, Harriet" he said. "Put her on."

There was a long pause while she connected the call. Once Mrs. Ivey came on the line, she started talking without bothering to say hello.

"Maude and I will be busy tomorrow, but we need to talk to you first thing Wednesday morning," she said. "There is something very important we must discuss."

He let out a loud sigh and switched the receiver to the other ear. If she didn't get to the point in a hurry, he'd have to sit down and rest.

He sidestepped toward the living room and stretched the phone cord to its full length. As hard as he pulled, it wasn't long enough to reach the chair.

"What da ya wanna talk about?"

"It isn't something I wish to discuss over the phone, Mr. Martin."

He scratched his head and switched the receiver to his other ear. Her late husband Robert wanted him to look out for her, but Mrs. Ivey could be downright aggravating. Just once he wished she'd come straight out and say what she wanted.

"Ya know, I'm gittin' too old fer this meetin' stuff."

"Nonsense," she said.

It was nonsense to her, but he was serious. She was always setting up meetings and expecting him to drop everything to be there. Maybe someday he'd work up the courage to say no.

"Mr. Martin?"

"I can't be late fer work, ya know."

"It won't take long," she said. "We'll have coffee waiting for you in the library."

Twelve

It was cozy and comfortable in my new bedroom. I wanted to sleep forever, but a warm breeze blowing in through the small gable window woke me up.

"Okay, Shirley," I said to myself. "You can't stay here forever."

I forced myself to get out of bed and stagger into my tiny bathroom. My poor, achy muscles screamed at me to stop moving, but I didn't listen. I started the shower.

After standing for several minutes under the hot water, my muscles relaxed, and my arms moved a lot freer. I turned off the shower, wrapped myself in a towel and combed my hair into its usual ponytail.

I wasn't sure what Grandma had planned for the day, so I dried off and threw on my old jeans and a baggy blouse. Then, I slipped into my new sandals and rushed downstairs.

Grandma and Aunt Maude were in the kitchen planning the schedule for the library. George was curled up on the floor under the table with his chin resting on Aunt Maude's mule slipper.

"I think being open two days a week should be sufficient," Grandma said.

"If you think so, Marie."

"I've called Mr. Martin," she said. "He'll be here tomorrow morning to help us."

"He works for Elaine now, Marie."

"We'll only take a few minutes of his time," she said. "I'm certain she'll understand."

"Should I bake some of my cookies?"

"That would be lovely, and we'll need several dozen more for the grand opening on Thursday."

They were so involved with their planning I didn't want to interrupt. I pulled out the chair next to Aunt Maude and sat down. My stomach grumbled at the sight of the half-eaten piece of toast on her plate.

"Good morning, Aunt Maude." I said.

She looked at me, but her mouth was stuffed full of toast. All she could manage was a nod.

"Good morning, dear," Grandma said.

She was at the sink dressed in her robe and slippers, rinsing out her coffee cup. The coffeepot was on the stove, washed and ready for the next day's breakfast.

"You looked especially tired last night," she said. "We didn't want to disturb you this morning."

"You're finished eating?"

"Yes, dear."

I leaned over the edge of the table and looked at George. He looked up at me and wagged his tail, but he didn't lift his chin off Aunt Maude's foot.

"You must be exhausted, too, big guy," I said. "Did you get your breakfast this morning?"

"He sure did," Aunt Maude said. "He's probably ready for his morning walk."

I stretched my arm out to him and scratched behind his ears. Just that simple motion reminded me how sore I was from moving and unpacking Aunt Maude's boxes.

After a few seconds, I stopped scratching him, groaned a little and sat back up. I was sure a little breakfast would help ease the pain, but I was too late for that.

Aunt Maude pushed her chair away from the table and stood up. She gathered her coffee cup and plate and walked them to the sink.

"I'll go get dressed now," Grandma said and wiped her hands on the dishtowel.

"I'll get ready, too," Aunt Maude said. "You take George to the backyard, Shirley."

"Don't be long, dear. We have a host of errands to run today."

They both walked to the back of the store and disappeared into the hallway. When I heard both apartment doors close, I almost felt abandoned.

"What's the big hurry?" I said to myself. "We have all day."

For some reason, Aunt Maude wanted me to take George out back instead of to his fire hydrant across the street. It was an odd request, but it wasn't my place to decide where he went for his walk.

I wanted to see the backyard anyway since I was too tired to check it out before I went to bed. I assumed it was overgrown and littered with trash the way the lot next to Grandma's old café used to be.

If it were a mess, I didn't know if my sore body was up to the challenge of cleaning it. All I could manage at that moment was a yawn.

"We'd better get going, George," I said. "We don't want to keep Grandma waiting."

While the little pug scooted out from under the table, I opened and closed cabinet drawers until I found his leash. It was still only a piece of clothesline with a loop at each end, but it worked just fine.

"Let's go, big guy."

George followed at my heel, and we made our way to the half-glass back door. I was going to attach the leash to his collar until I looked outside.

"Wow."

There wasn't a single weed anywhere, and the grass was mowed close to the ground. The entire lawn and several hardwood trees were surrounded by a wooden fence like the one at the café.

At the very back of the yard was a huge maple tree. Hanging from one of its limbs was the swing my grandpa made for me. Jim had somehow managed to relocate it from the old farmhouse and repaint it with a fresh coat of yellow.

"Wow, Jim."

I thought I gave up all my favorite things when Grandma sold her farmhouse, but I was wrong. Jim made sure my bedroom was perfect, and then, he remembered my swing.

"Oh, George," I said. "Let's go see."

I dropped the leash on the floor, threw the back door wide open, and we both bolted outside. While George sniffed every blade of grass, I sat down on my swing and pushed my feet against the ground.

When it swung with enough momentum, I picked up my feet and tucked my legs up under me. I leaned against the backrest and listened.

The ropes suspending the swing from the limb creaked as they rubbed against the bark. Just the way they did at the farmhouse.

"You better get that internship, Jim," I said. "You deserve it."

I closed my eyes and relaxed to the rhythm of the creaks. The familiar sound nearly lulled me to sleep until George let out a long series of yips. I'd never heard him yip that much at one time.

"Are you alright, big guy?"

I opened my eyes and looked around the yard for him. I finally saw him in front of a narrow gate in the back corner of the fence. He stood in his bulldog-like stance and stared at something beyond the gate.

"What is it, George?"

I untucked my legs, jumped to the ground and ran over to him. When I knelt down and laid my hand on his back, he stopped yipping and looked up at me.

"Did you see something out there?"

While I ran my hand along the streak of black hair on his back, I peeked through a narrow gap in the boards. There wasn't any sign of a squirrel or a chipmunk, but there was movement behind a juniper bush a few yards away.

Since I didn't bring the leash, I wrapped my arms around the little pug, held him close to my chest and stood up. I eased the gate open and whispered in his ear.

"Let's go see what's out there."

He wagged, lifted his head and gave my chin a sloppy kiss. I didn't have a free hand to wipe my face, so I gave him a big hug instead.

"I love you, too, big guy."

Thirteen

George stayed quiet in my arms while I pushed my way through the tall grass beyond the fence. I had to zigzag around thistles and several trees before I stopped a few feet from the juniper bush. Its branches no longer moved, but I could make out a silhouette behind it.

"Hello," I said. "Who's there?"

There was no reply, but George's tail wagged. I walked a little closer to the bush and stopped again.

"It's okay," I said. "You can come out now."

"Does he bite?"

The voice sounded like a young girl. Maybe it was my imagination but her voice sounded familiar.

"No," I said. "He doesn't bite."

"You sure?"

"Yes, I'm sure."

Just when I thought she wouldn't show herself, the little girl stepped out from behind the bush. She was wearing a faded sundress and scuffed leather shoes.

Her long dark braids hung over her shoulders and down the front of her dress. Her face was smudged with dirt from her forehead to her chin, and she didn't smile. She just stared at George and me with her big brown eyes.

"Hi, I'm Shirley."

"I know."

"You know who I am?"

She stepped a little closer to me and stretched her hand out to George. He sniffed her hand, licked her fingers and snorted.

"That tickles," she said and pulled her hand away.

"He likes you."

"He does?"

"Sure," I said. "He doesn't snort at just anybody."

She laughed at that, and George wiggled so hard I couldn't hold on to him. I put him on the ground, and he nosed his way to her through the tall grass.

When he reached her, he bumped into her leg and stopped. She giggled and bent over to pet his back.

"He's really cute," she said. "What is he?"

"He's a pug," I said. "His name's George."

"You're sure lucky to have a dog."

"Oh, he's not mine."

"Huh?"

"He's Aunt Maude's. My mom won't let me have a dog."

"Your mom?" she said. "What about your father?"

I didn't know why she wanted to know so much about me, but I didn't mind. Somehow, it was easy to talk to someone younger than I was.

"My dad passed away when I was a baby," I said. "It's just my mom and I."

"Just like Mama and me."

The little girl stood up and looked me in the eye. She didn't smile, and I wondered how someone so young could look so serious.

"Your dad's gone, too?" I said.

"Yeah, but he's not dead or anything."

"What do you mean?"

"He went away, and me and Mama moved here."

"What do you mean he went away?"

She reached down and stroked George's back again. It was obvious she did it to avoid looking at me.

"I don't know where he is," she said. "Mama says he's never coming back."

"I'm sorry."

It was all I could think to say. What does anybody say to a little girl whose father abandoned her?

"I don't remember seeing you in town before," I said.

"We moved off the farm a couple of weeks ago."

There was something very familiar about the girl, but I couldn't place her. If she and her mother had ever eaten at Ivey's Café, I would have remembered.

"George is really nice."

"He really is," I said, "Now that he's met you, he'll always remember who you are."

"Really?"

"Really."

I watched her and George until my stomach growled again. Without thinking, I slapped my hand against the waistband of my jeans.

"Oh, boy," I said. "I didn't get any breakfast."

"Me neither."

I looked at my watch. It was almost nine o'clock. I was old enough to take care of myself, but a little girl? I wondered where her mother was and why she hadn't fed her daughter.

The little girl stopped petting George and stood up. Her eyes were open wide, and she wore her serious expression again.

"I have to go," she said. "Mama's waiting for me."

"Where is your mother?"

Without answering me, she spun around and ran deep into the stand of trees. After a few seconds, she stopped running and turned around.

"You didn't tell me how you know who I am," I said.

"I'm Cindy," she said. "You saved my life."

Of course, that's why her voice was familiar. She was the little girl I helped off the dive platform at Lake Sullivan. The last time I saw her, she was on shore, frightened and shivering from the cold.

"You can come see George anytime," I said. "By the way, Grandma's having a grand opening for her library on Thursday."

"She has a library?"

"She sure does, and there are tons of books to read."

"Does she have comic books?"

"I don't know."

I was pretty sure Grandma didn't stock comic books, but I didn't want to discourage her from coming to the library. Before I could say more, she turned around and ran out of sight among the trees.

"Well, big guy," I said. "She must be in a big hurry."

I scooped the little pug into my arms and gave him a huge hug. He pressed his body against mine and relaxed his head against my chest.

"Maybe she'll come visit you again sometime."

My stomach rumbled again, but the noise didn't seem to bother George. He stayed relaxed in my arms until we were back inside the fenced yard.

As soon as I closed the gate behind us, he wriggled to get free. I set him on the ground, and he followed at my heel to the back door.

"Let's go see what's going on, okay?"

"Yip."

I held the door open for him, and he led me all the way to the kitchen. Grandma and Aunt Maude were seated at the table with their purses in their laps.

"Finally, young lady," Grandma said. "We're ready to leave."

She was wearing her navy blue dress with the white lace collar and her sensible laced shoes. As usual, her grey hair was pulled into a neat bun at the nape of her neck.

Aunt Maude was wearing her everyday housedress and her brown leather pumps. Her grey-peppered hair was braided across the top of her head, and she wore a wide smile.

Grandma, on the other hand, glared at me. It didn't take a genius to know she was angry with me for keeping her waiting.

"Get your purse," she said. "We want to arrive in Monticello before the fresh produce is picked over."

I wanted to go change out of my old jeans, but I knew she wouldn't allow me the time. Thankfully, I had on my good sandals and my hair was combed.

"What do we do about George?" I said.

"Don't worry," Aunt Maude said. "Bill Spencer will come and check on him."

With that detail covered, I hurried to the hooks by the front door and grabbed my purse. Without another word, Grandma and Aunt Maude got up from the table, walked right past me and out the door.

The smell of toast still lingered in the air, and my stomach let out another growl. I looked down at George.

"After last summer, you'd think I'd know better," I said. "If I don't want to starve, I can't sleep in late."

The little pug seemed unconcerned about my empty stomach and waddled over to the potbellied stove. After he plopped down on his blanket, I knelt next to him and scratched behind his ears.

"You be a good boy," I said. "We'll be back soon."

I gave him a kiss on the top of his head, stood up and walked to the front door. Before I closed and locked it behind me, I heard George snoring.

For him to fall asleep that fast was a sure sign he felt at home, and I didn't need to worry. He'd be just fine until Mr. Spencer came to feed him lunch.

Fourteen

Shopping at Woolworth's with Grandma and Aunt Maude was a life-changing experience. I never knew it could take so long for two people to agree on how many paper napkins to buy.

A patient sales clerk finally stepped in and mediated their every purchase for the grand opening. Without her help, we might have been stuck in Monticello until supper time.

As it was, the blue plate special we ate at the Woolworth's lunch counter didn't satisfy my hunger. My stomach never stopped growling the entire time I shopped for my own supplies.

"Okay, okay, stomach," I said under my breath. "I'll feed you if we ever get home."

After Woolworth's, Grandma and Aunt Maude agonized over what groceries to buy. They reacted the same way at the meat market and the dairy.

By the time they finished shopping, the bed of Grandpa's truck was just roomy enough to hold all the paper bags. Thankfully, we didn't need to put any inside the cab. There was only enough space in there for the three of us to sit.

"Well," Grandma said. "I believe we have everything we need."

She looked across the seat at Aunt Maude and me and nodded. I was afraid she might think of something else to buy, so I didn't ask her if she were sure.

"Let's go," Aunt Maude said. "George will be worried we're never coming home."

I was tempted to thank her for making that suggestion. Instead, I started the engine and drove out of town before either of them changed her mind.

Except for several curves around fields and a few hills, the trip back to Willowdale was boring. To keep myself alert, I rolled down my window and let fresh air blow in on my face. It helped a little.

After a few more minutes, I caught a glimpse of the water tower poking its head above the trees in Willowdale. The bright lettering on its side made me smile.

I slowed down when I turned off the main road onto the graveled county road leading to town. The last thing we needed was dust all over the bags in the back of the truck.

"We're almost there," I said.

When there wasn't a response, I glanced over at the two of them. Aunt Maude's eyes were closed, and her head rested on Grandma's shoulder. Grandma's head was leaned against the passenger window, and she snored softly.

"At least somebody got some rest," I said.

I nudged Aunt Maude's arm, and she jolted awake. She sat up straight, cleared her throat and elbowed Grandma.

"Wake up, Marie, we're home."

The second I pulled into the parking space in front of the store, I turned off the engine. I grabbed the keys, jumped out of the cab and stretched my arms out as wide as they would reach.

"Hallelujah," I said. "We're back."

Grandma ignored me, but Aunt Maude chuckled a little. She maneuvered her legs around the shift lever, scooted under the steering wheel and eased out of the driver's door.

"Let's get this thing unloaded, Shirley," she said. "George is waiting for us."

Grandma stepped out of the opposite side of the truck and walked up to the store's front door. While Aunt Maude and I loaded our arms with the lightest bags, she pulled up the corner of the doormat and found the key.

When she opened the door, George was standing just inside, his tail wagging. He greeted us with a loud yip and a very messy snort.

"Hi, big guy."

"That's my boy."

"I'll feed him," Grandma said.

Aunt Maude and I went inside and set the bags on the kitchen table. While she unpacked them and Grandma fed George, I went outside for the rest of them.

When I walked to the back of the truck, I was surprised to find Cindy standing there. This time, she was wearing jeans and a striped T-shirt. They were torn and faded but clean. Even her face was scrubbed.

"Can I help?" she said.

"You absolutely can," I said. "This particular bag is one I think you'd like to carry."

I handed her the bag with my Woolworth's purchases in it. After she peeked inside, she looked up at me and smiled.

"Really?"

"Really."

I loaded my arms with the last of the bags, and Cindy followed me inside. While I set the bags on the kitchen table, she kicked off her shoes and curled up on the closest sofa. The Woolworth's bag was on the cushion beside her.

"Who's the little girl?" Aunt Maude said.

"That's Cindy," I said. "She and her mother just moved to Willowdale, and I think she wants to check out Grandma's library."

Grandma picked up George's empty bowl, rinsed it in the sink and turned to look at Cindy. She frowned and shrugged her shoulders.

"We don't officially open until Thursday, but I suppose there's no harm in a small preview."

Grandma and Aunt Maude walked over to the sitting area and sat on the sofa closest to the bookcases. I walked over to Cindy on the other sofa, sat down next to the Woolworth's bag and took a deep breath.

"I've been thinking a lot about arranging an area in the library just for young readers."

"That sounds very interesting, dear," Grandma said.

"For my plan to work, I'll need two shelves for the books they'll love to read."

"I believe we can rearrange the shelves to accommodate your idea."

"It should be good practice to get me ready to become a teacher, don't you think?"

"I agree," she said. "Go on."

Telling Grandma my plan made me more nervous than I'd ever been in my life. She wanted to know details, but I was afraid of how she would react. I took another deep breath and forged ahead.

"Okay, Cindy," I said. "Why don't you pull out one of the books in the sack and show my grandma?"

"Which one?"

"It doesn't really matter," I said. "You choose."

She jammed both of her arms inside the bag and pulled out the most colorful comic book I bought. Her smile was nearly as wide as her face, and I could see the excitement in her eyes.

"This looks like a good one," she said.

Grandma squirmed a little, yanked her lace hankie from under her belt and dabbed at perspiration on her forehead. She cleared her throat and glared at me.

"Young lady," she said. "When our guest has gone home, you and I have a great deal to discuss."

Fifteen

After Cindy left and Aunt Maude went to the kitchen, the room turned quiet. Grandma and I didn't move from the sofas, and I could see she was struggling for the right words.

"I don't know what in the world you plan to do with those horrible things."

She looked over at the bag of comic books and wrinkled her nose. I knew they didn't fit in with her huge inventory of quality books, but that was my whole point.

"It'll be fine, Grandma," I said. "I plan to lure kids to your library with things they already love to read."

"Ye gods and little fishes," she said. "I would never have expected you to include comic books."

To her, reading anything less than the classics was an affront to authors and book lovers everywhere. Maybe she thought all children were raised the way I was.

"I need to design the shelves my way."

"Comic books?"

"I'll include the classics, too," I said. "First, I have to get the kids inside the door."

"Ye gods, why wouldn't they come in?"

"I'm afraid there might be more like Cindy," I said. "I don't think she's ever been inside a library."

"Good heavens, how is that even possible in this day and age?" she said. "Don't schools teach children anything important anymore?"

I didn't know anything about the school system in Willowdale, but I knew Cindy just moved to town. Maybe other farm kids didn't have good books to read or libraries to visit either.

"Don't worry, Grandma," I said. "Once I get them here, I'll introduce them to other books."

"I should certainly hope so, young lady."

I understood her perspective. When Mom and I had visited her and Grandpa for Thanksgiving and Christmas holidays, our only source of entertainment was reading. Books were Grandma's passion, and she refused to compromise her beliefs.

When Aunt Maude bought the first television set in town, Grandpa wanted to buy one for the farmhouse. He thought his grandchildren would enjoy it.

"Not my grandchildren," Grandma had said. "Whatever is this world coming to?"

I knew there was no sense trying to reason with her. I needed to design my young readers' shelves first and sell her on the idea later.

"Leave those awful things right there in the bag," she said. "You have something more important to do right now."

"Yes, Grandma."

She eased off the sofa, jammed her hankie under her belt and stomped away. Just like in an old comic book I once read, I could almost see steam shooting out of her ears.

When she was in the kitchen with Aunt Maude, I looked over at the shelves I wanted to arrange. I was anxious to get started on my project, but it would have to wait.

I reached into my Woolworth's bag and pulled out the multi-colored construction paper and the black marking pen I bought. I laid the pen down and spread the sheets of paper across the coffee table.

"This should make plenty of posters."

Before I started to write, George wandered over to his bed by the potbellied stove. He spun around three times on his rumpled blanket and plopped down on top of the mess.

"I don't care, big guy," I said to him. "No matter what Grandma says, I'm going to arrange my shelves my way."

Sixteen

"Have another cup of coffee, Mr. Martin," Aunt Maude said.

When he held his cup up for her, she refilled it with the last of the coffee. Then, she set the empty pot on the table and sat down on the sofa next to Grandma.

I looked at my empty cup and thought about going to the kitchen to make more hot chocolate. Somehow that seemed like too much work, and I decided one cupful was enough for me.

"I'm not gittin' any younger, ya know," Mr. Martin said. "Puttin' up posters is a lotta work."

While he gulped his coffee, Grandma and Aunt Maude looked over at me. They didn't need to say anything. I practically read their minds and forced myself to smile.

"It's okay, Mr. Martin," I said. "I'll help."

I was really too tired to be much help to anybody. I stayed up long after Grandma and Aunt Maude went to bed to finish the posters and my shelves.

I glanced at the nearest bookcase and let out a loud sigh. Two of the lower shelves were filled with my reading project, and I was proud of my work. I hoped the kids would think the books I chose were as much fun as I did.

Before I had a chance to ask Grandma what she thought of my project, she stood up. She brushed out wrinkles in her skirt and tucked a strand of hair back into the bun at the nape of her neck.

"That settles that," she said. "When you're finished, Mr. Martin, you may go to work at the café."

"Yes, ma'am."

"Shirley, I'll expect you back in time for breakfast."

"Yes, Grandma."

I was exhausted from lack of sleep, but I felt a little better when she included me in her breakfast plans. Taping up posters around downtown wouldn't take long, and my stomach growled at the thought of food.

"Well?" Grandma said. "Why are you two still here?"

Mr. Martin set his cup on the table and pushed himself off the sofa. He picked up about half of the posters off the coffee table and shuffled to the front of the store.

While he retrieved his old felt hat from one of the coat hooks, I stood up and grabbed the rest of the posters. I spooled two rolls of masking tape over my wrists as if they were bracelets and joined him at the door.

"Don't take long, Shirley," Grandma said. "After breakfast, I may have more errands for you to run."

"Yes, Grandma."

Mr. Martin opened the door with his free hand, and I rushed outside ahead of him. The door closed behind us before Grandma could think of anything more for us to do.

We stood on the sidewalk for a few seconds, looking up and down Main Street. It was too early for the stores to open, and there was no one in sight. The only traffic was a single car parked in front of the beauty shop.

"I gotta hurry," Mr. Martin said. "Miss Carter'll be ta work real soon."

"Remember, Grandma wants a poster on every store window," I said. "And don't forget the lamp posts."

He nodded and grumbled under his breath. Hanging posters was a major disruption in his normal schedule, and I knew he wasn't happy about it.

"It's okay, Mr. Martin," I said. "You only need to worry about that side of the street. I'll take care of this side."

He grumbled something else I couldn't understand. That time I ignored him and handed him a roll of tape.

"Thanks for your help."

He didn't bother to grumble again or say anything. He took the tape, stepped off the curb and headed toward the stores on the opposite side of the street.

His rudeness didn't bother me. He was just being his usual grumpy self.

After I watched him hang the first poster, I turned around and ran up the street to the bank. I had to rush if I didn't want to miss breakfast again.

Inside the bank's post office lobby, I taped one poster on the wall beside the locked mailboxes. I taped another on the bank's main door and a third on the glass door facing the street. Each poster was a different color to help attract more attention to the message written on them.

"Most everybody in town will see these," I said to myself. "Who doesn't go to the bank or pick up their mail?"

When I opened the glass door to leave, I saw Cindy staring at me from across the street. She stood next to George's favorite fire hydrant, kicking the toe of her shoe against the base of the yellow-colored metal.

"Cindy," I said. "Are you alright?"

The little girl smiled, stopped kicking the hydrant and darted across the street toward me. I held my breath when she didn't look in either direction for cars.

"You can't just run into traffic like that," I said.

She jumped onto the sidewalk and stopped beside me. Her smile was gone and her breathing was labored.

"I'm sorry, Shirley," she said. "I won't do that again."

"I should hope not."

She looked at the posters and tape I was holding. I couldn't blame her for being curious, and I wanted to do something to make up for my yelling at her.

"Would you like to help me?" I said.

"Do what?"

I held the posters out to her, and she took them from me. Her smile was back and her breathing sounded normal.

"You hold on to those and hand them to me one at a time," I said. "I'll put the tape on them."

"What are they?"

"They're announcements for tomorrow's grand opening."

"Grand opening for what?"

"Grandma's library," I said. "I told you it'd be opening on Thursday."

"Oh, yeah."

She wrapped her arms around the posters, held them close to her chest and followed me down Main Street. One at a time, she held up a poster while I taped it to a window or a lamp post.

When we reached Earl's garage and filling station at the end of the street, we taped the last two posters to the windows. There wasn't a single building or post on our side of the street without at least one piece of construction paper on it.

I looked across the street to check on Mr. Martin, but he was nowhere in sight. I could see he hadn't put up as many posters as Cindy and I had. Even so, there were enough of them to catch everyone's attention.

"Well, Cindy, it looks like we're done."

"Now, what?" she said.

I thought she would run away as usual, but she didn't. She stood her ground, and I didn't know what to do.

"Thanks for all your help," I said.

I thought a thank you was what she wanted, but she didn't leave. She stayed next to me and scuffed the sole of her shoe against the edge of the curb.

"That was fun," she said.

"Yes, it was, but I told Grandma I'd be right back."

"Okay."

"Don't you have some place you need to be?"

"No."

I studied her face to make sure she was alright. I was happy to see there was color in her cheeks, and she wasn't struggling to get a breath.

"Are you alright now?"

"I'm okay," she said. "Why?"

"Oh, no reason."

Cindy was a mystery to me, but I didn't want to pry. If she wanted to tell me something, I figured she'd let me know when she was ready.

"I have to get back to the store," I said. "You want to go with me?"

"Can I?"

"Of course, but Aunt Maude might make you eat some of her pancakes."

She dropped her chin to her chest and kicked at the curb again. When she looked up, she wore a smile, and her big brown eyes sparkled.

"That'd be okay, I guess."

"Maybe you should go tell your mother where you're going."

Cindy glanced at something across the street. Then, she turned toward me, jutted her chin upward and smiled even wider.

"She won't mind."

I doubted her mother wouldn't mind where she went, but I didn't have the time to ask her about it. Grandma and Aunt

Maude were waiting, and I didn't want them to eat without me.

"Okay," I said. "Let's go."

I walked as fast as I could up the sidewalk, and Cindy didn't have trouble keeping up with me. She half-ran, half-skipped beside me all the way to the store.

Seventeen

Elaine lowered herself onto the chair at the front table where Mr. Ivey used to sit. The green cushion it once had was too faded and too worn for her liking. Once the café purchase was complete, it was the first item she threw away.

"Perhaps I should consider new cushions for all of the chairs," she said to herself. "My customers might prefer that to sitting on bare wood."

She picked up her pencil and wrote the idea on the pad of paper in front of her. Since her only customer was Clyde Wilson drinking coffee, she ignored him and looked around the dining room for inspiration.

After a few minutes, she felt like an author with writer's block. There was only the one idea written on the pad, and no other ideas jumped out at her.

"Well, this is a monumental waste of my time," she said under her breath. "I must get ready for the reporter's arrival."

She pushed herself up from the table, gathered the paper and pencil and laid them on a shelf under the counter. Without a word to Clyde, she hurried to the kitchen.

Irene was at the sink, washing and rinsing dishrags and dishtowels. After she wrung the water from each one, she tossed it into an aluminum dishpan on the counter.

"When you finish hanging those on the line," she said, "I believe Clyde would like another cup of coffee."

"Yes, Miss Carter."

Her cook didn't look up and speak to her directly, but she ignored the rude behavior. The newspaper reporter was scheduled to arrive in five minutes, and she didn't have the time to worry about manners.

"You will be in charge of the café while the reporter is here," she said. "Do you understand?"

"Yes, Miss Carter."

"If you have any problems, I'll address them once the reporter is gone."

"Yes, Miss Carter."

"By the way, Irene, where is Mr. Martin?"

The cook twisted around and looked back at her. Her face showed no emotion.

"He's out back, throwin' out some trash."

"What kind of trash?"

"I think it's leftovers from somethin' Marie had him do."

"What?" she said. "He no longer works for that woman."

Irene twisted back around without saying another word and picked the aluminum pan off the counter. Before she could ask for more details about her handyman, the girl pushed past her and out the back door.

"Well, now," she said. "I'll just have to see what Mr. Martin is really up to."

She stomped toward the new gift shop at the back of the café and stood just inside its door. A quick look around told her everything was neatly in place.

"At least my store and gift shop are ready for the reporter," she said, jamming her fists on her hips. "If only my employees were as cooperative."

She hurried to the back door, threw it wide open and walked out onto the back steps. When she saw Irene and Mr. Martin, she realized she was already too late.

While Irene hung towels and rags from the clothesline, Mr. Martin stood near the steps, staring at the incinerator barrel. A ribbon of smoke and bits of black ash rose from it.

"What are you doing, Mr. Martin?"

"Burnin' the trash, Miss Carter," he said.

She rushed down the steps and leaned over the side of the metal barrel. There was nothing left in it for her to see but a little smoke and a mound of charred rubble.

When she looked up at Mr. Martin, he grinned, tipped his old felt hat at her and walked away. Without evidence, she'd never know what job he had done for Marie when he was supposed to be at the café.

Eighteen

I stepped outside and sat on the bench in front of the window. As always, Aunt Maude's buttermilk pancakes were light and fluffy, and the bacon was fried light brown and crisp. Everything was perfect except for Cindy.

She rushed out after eating without a thank you, and I wondered what was wrong with her mother. Just because they once lived on a farm was no excuse not to teach her daughter to be polite.

"Who do you suppose her mother is anyway?" I said to myself.

"Shirley, are you alright?"

Grandma came outside and sat on the bench beside me. The front of her bib apron was wet from washing the breakfast dishes.

"I'm okay, Grandma," I said. "I'm just sorry Cindy was rude to you and Aunt Maude."

Grandma reached over and patted my hand. She didn't seem to be the least bit upset.

"You must understand, dear," she said. "Sometimes manners are the least of our concerns."

What was that supposed to mean? Cindy took advantage of her and Aunt Maude's generosity, and I was angry with her.

"I don't understand that at all, Grandma."

"Life is often hardest on the young," she said. "Sometimes we expect more from them than they are capable of giving."

That didn't help. My mom always expected me to mind my manners and do as I was told. Why shouldn't I hold Cindy to the same standard?

"Do you even know Cindy's mother or where they live?" Grandma said.

"I asked her about that, but she wouldn't tell me."

"I'm not a bit surprised."

She stood up, untied her apron and folded it on the seat of the bench. After she brushed out wrinkles in her dress, she tucked a loose strand of hair into the bun at her neck.

"I believe it's time we make a friendly call on our newest neighbors."

"Who are our new neighbors?"

"Come along," she said. "You have already met one of them."

Before I could ask who that person was, she turned and hurried up the sidewalk. I jumped up from the bench and practically ran to catch up to her.

At the middle of the block, we waited for traffic and crossed the street when it was clear. Several of the drivers honked their horns and waved at us. I waved back at them but not Grandma. She acknowledged them with a single nod of her head.

On the other side of the street, we walked up to the front door of Kut and Kurl. I knew Grandma didn't have an appointment, but I wasn't about to ask her why we were there.

When we went inside, a young woman walked up to us. Her dark wavy hair hung to her shoulders, and she wore a wide smile. Her resemblance to Cindy was startling.

"I'm Mrs. Ivey, and this is my granddaughter Shirley," Grandma said. "I heard we had a new hairdresser in town."

"I'm Sarah Thomas," she said. "It's nice to meet you."

She shook Grandma's hand. Then, she took my hand and shook it. I guessed she wasn't any older than Irene, and shaking her hand felt awkward.

"It's nice to meet you, too," I said.

I didn't know why Grandma wanted me to meet her, but I was glad I did. I liked her immediately.

"I'm happy to finally meet you, Shirley," she said. "Cindy talks about you all the time."

"Cindy?"

"My daughter," she said. "She practically idolizes you."

"She thinks I saved her life," I said. "I didn't really do anything special."

"Of course you did, and she wants to grow up to be just like you."

I felt my face turn red. I knew Cindy followed me around a lot, but I had no idea she felt that way. I tried to think of a response, but I couldn't. Thankfully, Grandma spoke for both of us.

"You're busy," she said. "We won't keep you."

"Shirley," she said. "I know several popular hairdos you'd like if you ever decide to change your ponytail."

"I'll think about it."

I looked around the tiny beauty shop. There were only two other people in the room. One was a woman sitting under a hair dryer and another on a swivel chair in front of a wall mirror. I didn't know either of them, but they stared at Grandma and me the entire time.

"Thank you for stopping in," Sarah said, grabbing a comb from a glass jar. "I'm sorry Cindy wasn't up from her nap in time to see you."

"A nap?" I said.

Grandma wrapped her hand around my elbow and pulled me toward the front door. Her frown told me all I needed to know. Cindy's nap was none of my business.

"You and Cindy are welcome to stop by the store anytime," Grandma said. "The grand opening for my library is tomorrow."

"I saw your sign on the window," she said. "Thanks for letting us know."

"I have two shelves set up especially for the kids," I said.

Grandma practically shoved me out the door before I had a chance to say anything more. She waited until the beauty shop door was closed before she spoke again.

"Now you know, young lady," she said.

"What do I know?"

Grandma didn't answer me. Instead, I followed her across the street, and we stepped up onto the opposite sidewalk. She was so quiet I thought she hadn't heard my question, so I repeated it.

"What do I know, Grandma?"

She continued to walk without speaking. I didn't know how she knew about Sarah, but I knew there were no secrets in small towns. Like it or not.

When we reached her store, Grandma picked her apron off the bench. She went inside, talking to me over her shoulder.

"Now you know Cindy's mother," she said. "You also know she's young and works hard to rear her daughter on her own."

"Yes, Grandma."

"In case you didn't notice," she said, "Sarah and Cindy live in the backroom of the shop."

"I didn't realize—"

"No, you didn't realize," she said. "Next time, young lady, don't be so eager to judge someone before you understand their situation."

"I'm sorry, Grandma," I said. "I won't forget."

"Good."

She nodded at me, walked into the kitchen and draped her apron across the back of a chair. The television set in Aunt Maude's apartment blared out an episode of her favorite soap opera, and Grandma shook her head.

"Mark my words," she said. "Television will be the ruination of the world."

I already knew how she felt about televisions, so I didn't follow her into the kitchen. I walked over to the potbellied stove and plopped down on the floor next to George. The little pug was on his blanket, snoring softly.

"Do you think Sarah even has a way to cook for Cindy?" I said to him. "What about washing clothes or taking a bath?"

George rolled onto his back, but he didn't open his eyes. I ran my hand over his chest and watched his rib cage rise and fall.

"There's one thing I do know, big guy," I said. "I don't want Cindy's hero worship."

Jim and I helped the lifeguard get a lot of people to shore the day of the storm. We did what needed to be done, and that was all there was to it.

"What am I going to do, George?" I said. "I can't have her thinking I'm special when I'm not."

Nineteen

"The Sunday school class thought you should have this."

Pastor Lawrence came inside the store with a thick roll of white butcher paper in his hands. I took the roll from him, and Aunt Maude handed him a mug of steaming coffee.

"What is it you have there, Albert?" she said.

"The children made a banner for today's grand opening," he said. "They insisted I bring it over here first thing this morning."

It was only six o'clock, but he was already dressed for work in his navy blue slacks and black dress shoes. He was unusually casual with his short-sleeved shirt unbuttoned at the collar and no tie.

"Let's see what they made," I said.

I put the roll on the floor, stepped on one end of the paper and kicked the roll with my other foot. When the banner was fully unrolled, it stretched all the way from the door to the wall with the mailbox cabinet. Along its full length was the word "WELCOME" printed with red crayons.

"It was very thoughtful of them," Grandma said. "Don't you think so, Maude?"

"I guess so."

"We must be certain to write a nice thank you note to the class."

"But it's so—long," Aunt Maude said. "Where can we hang it?"

We all stood quietly and studied the banner. There wasn't a wall in the store large enough to hold it.

"You have to hang it somewhere," the pastor said. "You can't disappoint the children."

He stood next to me, sipped his coffee and shook his head. Grandma and Aunt Maude eased onto the brocade chairs by the stove and put their feet up on the footstools.

"There must be a place for it, Marie," Aunt Maude said.

"There must be."

For several minutes, the only sounds in the room were George's snoring and the ticking clock in the kitchen. As the seconds clicked by, I wasn't confident any of us would come up with a good idea.

Just when I thought the banner ruined all of our careful decorating plans, there was a knock on the front door. I ran to answer it, grateful for the interruption.

"Morning, Shirley."

Mr. Spencer stood outside the door holding a rectangular board almost as tall and as wide as he was. I couldn't imagine what it was for, but I didn't think it was polite to ask.

"Good morning, Mr. Spencer," I said. "We're not quite ready to open yet."

"Good," he said. "I brought something for Marie and Aunt Maude."

Nothing about the day was going as planned. We didn't need another complication, but I couldn't leave him standing outside.

"Come in," I said. "We're just discussing our plans."

I held the door for him while he carried the board inside and leaned it against the wall. The front side of it was facing away from the room, so I couldn't see what was on it.

He walked over to Pastor Lawrence and shook his hand. Then, he looked down at the banner on the floor.

"Well, now," he said. "What do we have here?"

"I'm afraid we have a dilemma," the pastor said.

While Pastor Lawrence explained the banner to him, Aunt Maude pushed herself up from the chair. She went straight to the kitchen and opened a cupboard door.

"Who else wants coffee?" she said.

Like children in front of their teacher, everyone raised his hand except me. I couldn't stand the taste of the stuff.

She grabbed three more mugs from the cupboard and the coffeepot from the stove. She put it all on a tray, carried the tray into the main room and set it on the empty stool.

Once she filled the three mugs, Grandma and Mr. Spencer each took one. She picked up the last one and sat back down on her chair.

"More coffee, Pastor?" I said.

When he nodded at me, I picked up the pot and poured the last of the coffee into his mug. I didn't know what else to do to help, so I took the empty pot to the kitchen and set it in the sink.

"I know you're right in the middle of something," Mr. Spencer said. "I just came over to find out what you named your store."

Grandma and Aunt Maude looked at each other, then at Mr. Spencer. It never occurred to me they hadn't chosen a name.

"What do you think, Maude?"

"I'm not sure, Marie," she said. "What do you think?"

Could the day get any worse? The first thing anyone at the grand opening would want to know is the store's name. What was I supposed to tell them?

I went back into the main room and watched Grandma and Aunt Maude struggle with their decision. If they couldn't decide where to hang the banner, how could they ever decide on something as important as a name?

"If you don't mind," Mr. Spencer said. "I'd sure like to show you something."

"Can't it wait?" I said. "I don't think Grandma or Aunt Maude can handle anything else."

"It can't wait," he said. "It's just what they both need right now."

He put his coffee mug on the tray and walked over to the board he brought. As he carried it over to Grandma and Aunt Maude, he held the front of it close to his body. I still couldn't see what was on it.

"Hope you don't mind," he said. "I made you a new sign for your store."

"Another sign?" Aunt Maude said. "It's too big for in here, don't you think?"

"It hangs outside, so everybody knows what to call this place."

"How is that possible," Grandma said. "Maude and I haven't even come to a consensus on a name."

"Oh, I have a pretty good idea what you're going to call it."

At first, he turned the board around so only they could see the other side. Grandma's mouth dropped open and Aunt Maude' eyes filled with tears.

When he turned it around for the rest of us to see, I had to laugh. He had routed the most obvious name for the store across the face of the board.

"It's perfect, Mr. Spencer."

"Ye gods and little fishes," Grandma said. "Why didn't we think of that?"

Aunt Maude pulled a hankie from under the sleeve of her housedress and blew her nose. The sound was so loud Grandma cringed a little, but she didn't say anything.

"What're we waiting for?" Mr. Spencer said. "I'll back my truck up, and we'll hang this thing where it belongs."

"Back up your truck?" Grandma said. "Whatever for?"

"You'll see in a minute."

He leaned the board against the wall, opened the front door, and Grandma and Aunt Maude followed him outside. I stayed behind and grabbed George's leash off the hook by the door.

The little pug was sound asleep, so I knelt down and scratched him behind his ears. When he opened his eyes, I secured the leash to his collar.

"Come on, big guy," I said. "You need to watch this."

He got up, shook his body and wagged his tail. As soon as I stood up, he followed me to the front door.

"Here, Pastor Lawrence," I said and handed him the leash.

"What am I supposed to do with this?"

"Take George outside with you," I said. "I'll be out in a couple of minutes."

He put his mug on the coffee table, opened the front door and led George outside. When the door closed behind them, I walked back to the pantry.

I searched every shelf until I found the wooden box Grandpa used to store under the café counter. I placed the box on the only empty shelf in the room and opened the lid. Inside was Grandpa's American flag, folded neatly and wrapped in white tissue paper.

"It's the perfect time to hang this," I said to myself.

After removing the paper, I carried the folded flag to the front door. Maybe we couldn't decide where to hang the banner, but Grandpa's flag had its own place of honor.

When I walked outside, Grandma and Aunt Maude were standing on the sidewalk behind Mr. Spencer's truck. It was backed up, perpendicular to the walk, blocking potential traffic in both directions.

Pastor Lawrence was standing behind them with George right beside his feet. When he saw me, he picked up the little pug and moved over to give me room in front of the wooden dowel.

"Grandma," I said. "Can we do this first?"

When she turned around, her hands flew to her chest and her eyes grew wide. For a moment, she was speechless.

"Are you alright, Grandma?"

When she regained her composure, she lowered her hands and stood up as tall as she could. She smiled at me and held her chin up high.

"You do the honors, dear," she said.

I carefully unfolded the flag until I found the grommets along its edge. I slipped them over the hooks on the dowel, brushed out creases in the material and made certain it hung straight. When the flag looked its best, I stepped back and stood next to Grandma.

"I vowed I'd never forget all the family we've lost," I said. "I know they're with us in spirit today for your grand opening."

Grandma wrapped an arm around my waist, and I slipped an arm over her shoulder. For several seconds, we studied the flag that represented generations of our family and the sacrifices they made.

"Good idea, Shirley," Aunt Maude said. "Now, everybody knows the library's open."

Grandma seemed a little too quiet for such a special occasion. I was afraid I upset her until she looked up at me. Her smile was radiant.

"Yes, Robert would be proud his flag hangs here for our grand opening," she said. "He would be even more proud of his granddaughter for remembering its importance."

Twenty

Elaine stood at the café window, glaring at Mr. Spencer's truck. She folded her arms across her chest and tapped her toe against the wooden floor.

"Do you have any idea what they're doing over there?"

"Nope," Irene said, "Must be somethin' special with the flag up and all."

She looked over at her cook standing at the screen door and shook her head. Obviously, the girl didn't understand the situation. In the competitive world of business, it was imperative to know what the other stores were doing at all times.

"Certainly you can see Mr. Spencer's truck is impeding the flow of traffic."

Irene reached behind her head and pulled her braid over her shoulder. While she twisted the tip of it in her fingers, she looked up and down the street.

"I don't see any cars."

"That is completely beside the point, Irene," she said. "If a vehicle were to come along, its occupants wouldn't have access to my café."

"I suppose."

She knew there was no supposing about it. Marie and Maude were up to something without giving her proper notification. As a Willowdale business owner, she was within her rights to lodge a complaint.

Before she could call someone in authority, Mr. Spencer climbed out of the cab and into the bed of his truck. He stood at the tailgate with his back to the café.

"Of all things."

"What is it, Miss Carter?"

"He must see us watching him," she said. "He didn't even bother to acknowledge our presence."

"That's okay. He's kind of busy."

She was always amazed at how forgiving Irene and the other residents of the small town were. They simply refused to understand there was never a good excuse for rudeness.

She pulled a chair from the front table, dragged it to the window and sat down. If she had to watch the antics across the street, she wanted to be comfortable.

After a minute or two, she watched Shirley go into the store and bring out a large board. She walked over to the truck and lifted it up to Mr. Spencer.

"What do you imagine they're doing now?" she said.

Before Irene could answer, Marie and Maude walked past the truck and sat down on the bench. Pastor Lawrence followed behind them with Maude's dog on a leash.

After the two women sat down, the odd little dog spun in a tight circle at Maude's feet. Just when it appeared as though he would never stop spinning, he collapsed in a heap on the sidewalk.

"Isn't George just the cutest thing, Miss Carter?"

She knew there was no accounting for taste, and she took the girl's words seriously. If she didn't say something immediately, Irene's affection for the strange little dog could be a problem.

"Must I remind you, Irene?" she said. "Unlike Mrs. Ivey, I never permit dogs inside my café under any circumstance."

"Course not, Miss Carter."

The pastor didn't sit down with the women. He handed Maude the leash, jumped off the curb and got into his car. He backed the sedan out of the parking space, waved at them through the driver's window and drove out of sight.

"Where do you think he's going?"

"Probably to pick up Mr. Martin," Irene said.

"Yes, of course."

The group across the street talked back and forth, but their voices were too low to hear. She scooted her chair closer to the window and leaned forward on the seat.

Moving the chair didn't help, but she refused to go outside to listen. She didn't want Marie or Maude to know she was curious about their project.

"Is it okay if I go see what's goin' on?" Irene said.

She studied her cook's face and thought about her request. The idea was intriguing, and it fit perfectly into her long-term strategy.

"We aren't open yet," she said. "I see no reason why you shouldn't join your friends."

"Thanks, Miss Carter."

"I expect you to return in a few minutes."

"Yes, Miss Carter."

"On your way out," she said, "remove that hideous piece of construction paper from my window."

"Yes, Miss Carter."

Irene untied her grease-stained apron and threw it across the back of the nearest chair. She ran outside, letting the screen door slam shut, ripped down the poster and tossed it into the trash barrel beside the door.

Her cook's rough exit didn't surprise her. Growing up in Willowdale wasn't conducive to refined behavior.

"Her lack of manners is of little consequence at the moment," she said to herself.

Her first priority was to recruit someone to bring her information about the other businesses in town. Although Irene wasn't particularly articulate, everyone in town liked her. It was an advantage that could be exploited.

"Jim may not want to spy for me any longer," she said, "but I believe Irene will do quite nicely."

Twenty-one

"Come on up, Shirley," Mr. Spencer said. "I need your help."

I didn't know anything about hanging signs, but I wanted to do what I could. I stepped onto the hitch, threw my leg over the tailgate and climbed into the truck bed. As soon as I was settled, he handed me one end of the board.

"You hold that end up," he said. "I'll drive a nail in this end."

"Okay."

We held the sign against the beam holding up the front edge of the shed roof. When it was level and centered with the front door, Mr. Spencer pounded a nail through his end of the board.

The sign was heavy. I didn't know how long I could hold my end of it above my head.

"Can we work a little faster, Mr. Spencer?"

I didn't need to worry. He came right over to me and drove a nail through my end of the board and into the beam.

"That's just temporary," he said. "We'll use screws to hold it permanent."

I dropped my arms to my sides, shook them to get the blood flowing again and breathed a sigh of relief. I wasn't as much help as Jim would have been, but at least the sign was up.

"Shirley?"

I turned around and saw Irene standing on the sidewalk in front of the café. She gave me a quick wave, stepped off the curb and hurried across the street.

"What's goin' on?" she said. "I was watchin' from the café."

When I pointed to the sign, she looked up at it, and her smile disappeared. She didn't seem to notice Mr. Spencer standing in the truck right beneath it.

"Hey, Irene," he said. "What do you think?"

Instead of saying hello or giving him her opinion, she just stood and stared at the sign. It wasn't like her to be so quiet, and I started to worry.

I eased my legs over the side of the truck bed and jumped to the ground. I landed only a few feet from her, but she still didn't say anything.

"What's wrong?" I said. "Is it misspelled or something?"

Irene came as close to being a sister to me as anyone I knew. She always gave sound advice when I needed it, and I respected her opinion.

"It's nothin' like that," she said.

"Then, what?"

She walked up to me, and laid a hand on my shoulder. With the heel of her other hand, she wiped tears from her face.

"It's a real pretty sign," she said.

"Then why are you crying?"

"Because this is the way it's supposed to be."

"What do you mean?"

"Nothin'."

Irene never said anything without meaning to say it. What-ever was bothering her was definitely something.

Mr. Spencer leaned over the side of the truck and handed me the end of an extension cord. The other end was attached to the drill in his hand.

"Go plug that in, will you?" he said. "Have to get this thing hung right."

Irene dropped her hand from my shoulder and stepped back a few feet. She didn't say another word.

Mr. Spencer and I looked at each other and shrugged our shoulders. I didn't know what to say. For some reason, Irene was fixated on his sign.

"I'll go plug this in," I said to her. "Why don't you go sit with Grandma and Aunt Maude?"

She shook her head and stepped back another foot or so. I didn't know what was wrong, but at least she wasn't crying any more.

"Shirley," she said. "Clyde's got to know about this right away."

"You can show it to him after the café closes," I said. "It'll still be here."

"No, I got to tell him right now."

"Okay," I said. "Go use Grandma's phone."

"Won't do any good."

"Why not?"

"He's out paintin' the barn."

When she finally looked at me, I saw the concern in her eyes. She was the most even-tempered person in the world, and it wasn't like her to get upset.

"If it's that important," I said, "I can drive you wherever you need to go."

"You sure?"

"Of course, I'm sure."

I grasped my end of the extension cord in both hands and dragged it toward the store's front door. Irene didn't move or offer to help me.

"You wait right there, okay?" I said.

"I'm not goin' anywhere."

"Good."

I hurried inside, plugged the cord into the nearest outlet and grabbed the keyring from its hook by the door. When I went back outside, I walked over to Grandma and Aunt Maude.

"Irene needs a ride," I said, "and she needs to leave right now."

"Ye gods and little fishes," Grandma said. "Doesn't she realize our grand opening is about to begin?"

"I'm not sure, Grandma, but she's really upset about something."

"What in the world could be that urgent?"

"She didn't tell me, but she needs to talk to Clyde right away."

"She's welcome to use our phone," Aunt Maude said.

"I told her that, but Clyde can't get to a phone right now."

Aunt Maude touched Grandma's arm and nodded toward Mr. Spencer's truck. When Grandma and I looked in that direction, Irene was standing behind the tailgate with her braid in her hands. She twisted the end of it in her fingers and shifted her weight from one foot to the other.

"She only does that when she's thinking hard about something," Aunt Maude said.

"I'm well aware of that," Grandma said, "but her timing couldn't be worse."

"I already told her I'd give her a ride."

"You did, did you?"

Grandma stood up and looked me straight in the eye. I didn't know what she was thinking, but she didn't look happy.

"Alright, Shirley," she said. "You may take your grandpa's truck."

"Thank you."

"Remind Irene the café opens soon, and she's Elaine's only cook."

"Yes, Grandma."

"Once you've delivered her to her destination, return here immediately."

"Yes, Grandma."

I threw my arms around her neck and gave her a quick hug. When she didn't return my hug, I knew she was disappointed in me.

"I'll get back as soon as I can," I said.

"Make certain you do."

"Yes, Grandma."

It wasn't fair of me to leave her and Aunt Maude to handle the start of the grand opening alone. They were depending on my help, but right then, Irene needed me more.

"You drive careful," Aunt Maude said.

"I will."

I turned around and threw a quick wave in Mr. Spencer's direction. When I walked around the tailgate of his truck, Irene was no longer there. She was inside the cab of Grandpa's truck, waiting for me.

"Wow," I said under my breath. "This really must be important."

I climbed into the driver's side of the old truck and started the engine. After I shifted the gears into reverse, I looked over at Irene.

"Where are we going?" I said.

"Mr. Wilson's farm."

"Clyde's painting his dad's barn?"

"Yeah," she said. "He gettin' things ready."

"Getting ready for what?"

When she didn't answer, I grew more curious. Farmers around Willowdale were getting ready to harvest crops, not paint barns. I didn't understand why Clyde was.

I backed out of the parking space and drove west toward Cemetery Road. Mr. Wilson's farm was several miles from town, and it wouldn't be a quick trip.

His guard dog, Sebastian, would probably meet us in the driveway, but I tried not to worry. Jim assured me the collie would remember me and be friendly the next time I went there. Just in case his theory was wrong, Clyde would be there to help us.

Twenty-two

While I drove along Cemetery Road, I focused my attention on dodging endless potholes. Irene sat quietly on the other side of the cab. Her hands were folded in her lap, and her eyes were fixed on the road ahead.

"Maybe it's none of my business," I finally said, "but can't you tell me what Clyde's getting ready for?"

Irene's silence lasted a few more seconds. Then, she twisted in the seat and looked at me.

"Can you keep a secret?" she said.

"You know I can."

"He's sprucin' up the place for after our weddin'."

"You're getting married?"

"Yep, come Christmas."

I hadn't heard anything about a wedding. She was supposed to be my friend, and it hurt my feelings she didn't mention it to me.

"Why does he have to paint the barn?"

"Because we'll be livin' with Mr. Wilson, and Clyde wants the place lookin' nice for me."

I couldn't picture a new bride sharing a house with her father-in-law, but it wasn't any of my business. I just hoped the arrangement worked well for all of them.

"I guess you have everything all planned."

"Not really," she said. "Not much to plan."

"Why is that?"

"It'll be real small," she said. "Over to the justice of the peace in Monticello."

"You're eloping?"

"Yeah, I guess."

"That sounds romantic."

"Not really," she said. "Me and Clyde don't have any money."

I shook my head. That explained the living arrangements, but weddings only happened once in a girl's life. She shouldn't have to skimp on her big day.

"You could have Pastor Lawrence marry you at his church."

"Can't."

"Why not?"

"Clyde doesn't go to church."

Pastor Lawrence was a really nice man. I was pretty sure church attendance wasn't a prerequisite to marrying them. I wanted to reassure Irene of that, but she didn't ask for my opinion.

We drove another mile or two without speaking until I couldn't stand the silence any longer. I needed to know more.

"What's the matter with the new sign?" I said. "Something about it upset you."

"There's nothin' wrong with the sign."

"It didn't look that way to me.

126

She turned a little more toward me and pulled her braid over her shoulder. While she twisted the end of it in her fingers, she smiled her somewhat toothless smile at me.

"When I was little, I told Aunt Maude I wanted to get married in her general store."

"What did she say to that?"

"She said she'd be real proud if I did."

In spite of my hurt feelings, I couldn't help but smile. It sounded just like Aunt Maude to encourage a little girl's dream.

"Except she sold her store before you got engaged."

"Yep," she said. "My plan went up in smoke."

Nothing she said eased my confusion. It didn't come close to explaining why she was upset and needed to see Clyde.

"What does any of that have to do with the sign?"

"You're supposed to be the smart one," she said. "Don't you get it?"

"No."

Whatever was bothering her was still beyond my understanding. I guess I wasn't as smart as she thought.

"Don't you see?" she said. "I can have the weddin' I want after all."

I was tired from staying up too late. My brain was fuzzy and refused to track her logic. There seemed to be an important piece of the puzzle missing, and I couldn't figure it out.

"Come on, Shirley," she said. "Mr. Spencer's sign says it all."

I slapped the steering wheel, pulled the truck to the side of the road and slammed on the brakes. The cloud of dust behind the truck caught up to us and blew in through the open windows.

We both choked and tried to fan it away from our faces with our hands. When that didn't work, we stopped trying and started laughing until tears ran from our eyes.

"Why couldn't I think of that?" I said and slapped the steering wheel again.

I finally understood the significance of the words "General Store" on the sign, but something rubbed me the wrong way. If she changed her mind about eloping, she needed to rethink the whole plan.

"Why do you have to wait until Christmas to get married?"

"It's after harvest, and Clyde's got time."

Planning a wedding around harvest was the least romantic thing I had ever heard. All they needed was a little help from their friends to move the date up.

"What would you say to getting married before I leave for home?"

"What?"

"It's doable."

"How do you figure?" she said. "Aren't you leavin' real soon?"

"Let Grandma and Aunt Maude and I worry about the details," I said. "You concentrate on your dress and where you're going on your honeymoon."

"Honeymoon?" she said. "Me and Clyde don't have any money, remember?"

I had an idea about that, too, but I had to discuss it with Miss Carter first. She wouldn't be an easy sell.

Then, I needed help from everybody in town. If they pitched in like they did with annual potlucks, the reception would be a huge success.

"You're sure quiet, Shirley," she said. "What're you thinkin'?"

"I'm thinking I need to get you to the farm to tell Clyde he's getting married one week from Saturday."

"A week from Saturday?"

I pulled the truck back onto the road, and Irene twisted her braid a little faster. I couldn't blame her if she were nervous. I was the first person she told about her plans, and I wanted to change everything.

"Clyde's really going to be surprised when you tell him the good news."

"Uh-huh."

She didn't sound convinced, but I had no doubt Clyde would be okay with the new plan. All he had to do was get the marriage license and finish painting the barn.

"There's somethin' else," Irene said.

"What's that?"

"Will you be my maid of honor?"

"Oh, Irene," I said. "Of course, I will."

Twenty-three

"What's got ya so happy?"

Mr. Martin stood at the kitchen door and watched Irene flip a dozen hamburgers on the griddle. While they cooked, she added chopped onions, a raw egg, some ketchup and spices to a bowl full of ground sirloin.

She kneaded the mixture with her hands, pressed six more burgers and tossed them on the griddle. All the while, she grinned and hummed a nonsensical tune under her breath.

"Not gonna tell me, huh?"

"Nothin' to tell," she said. "I had a real nice ride with Shirley this mornin'."

She washed her hands at the sink, wiped them dry on her apron and turned around. She wasn't the kind to be pushed very far for information, so he kept quiet.

"Aren't you supposed to be sweepin' the floor?" she said.

"Don't ya worry none," he said. "I'm gittin' outa yer way."

He backed out of the doorway, walked over to the wall next to the tiny bathroom and yanked a broom off a hook. He already swept the dining room that morning, but nothing was ever good enough for Miss Carter. She wanted it swept again.

"There's no pleasin' that woman," he said to himself.

He started toward the front of the café, weaving around the tables in the dining room. The place was filled with a bus load of hungry passengers from Lafayette, and the noise from all their voices was deafening.

In the midst of it all, Miss Carter hustled from table to table taking orders and serving food. He gave her credit for working hard, but her service was a little slow.

"Gotta get some help," he said under his breath. "Yer gonna wear yerself to a frazzle."

When he was almost to the front of the room, a woman from the bus reached out and grabbed his shirt sleeve. He frowned at her, but he stopped to see what she wanted.

"Maybe you can tell me what's happening across the street," she said.

He looked at the front window. The poster he taped there was gone, but there were plenty more posted on both sides of the street. He wondered how anyone could miss seeing the announcement about the grand opening.

"It's the new library," he said. "Just opened taday."

"A library in this small town?" she said. "How fun."

He grunted a little, pulled his sleeve from her grasp and left the woman to eat her meal. He wasn't sure how much fun a library was, but if she thought so, it was good for Mrs. Ivey.

At the front of the dining room, he found several of the newspapers on the rack out of order. He stood the broom next to the door, straightened the papers and organized the magazines the way Mrs. Ivey used to like.

"That oughta do her," he said.

When he stood back to admire his work, a little girl in a striped T-shirt and faded jeans ran past the front window. She had something tucked under her arm. A few seconds later, a group of boys ran past going in her direction.

"What the devil?"

He stepped outside and watched the boys chase the girl up one side of Main Street and down the other. When she reached the front door of the General Store, she stopped running and flopped down on the curb.

Even from across the street, he could hear her cough and gasp for air. He didn't know what was wrong with her or why the boys chased her, but it looked like she needed help.

With no traffic to get in his way, he crossed the street and stood on the sidewalk behind the girl. The boys finally caught up to her, but they came to an abrupt halt when they saw him standing there.

"Hey, Mr. Martin," the oldest boy said.

"Hey, yerself."

"We're just trying to get that comic book back to Mrs. Ivey," he said. "Isn't that right, Cindy?"

The little girl took a deep breath and jumped to her feet. She tucked the comic book tighter under her arm and faced her accusers.

"It's mine," she said. "Shirley said I could keep it."

"There ya have it, boys," he said. "Ya got yer answer."

One of the older boys stepped forward. His hands were balled into tight fists, and he stared directly into his eyes.

"You're taking the word of a farm girl over ours?" he said.

"You betcha."

The youngest boy took a step forward and stuck his tongue out at Cindy. She answered him by sticking out her tongue at him.

He wanted to laugh at their childish maneuver, but he didn't want to spoil the moment for her. He was only the referee. She handled the problem her way.

"Git on home, now" he said. "I never wanna see ya botherin' Cindy agin."

The oldest boy leaned over and whispered something to the rest of the boys. They all spun around and ran up the sidewalk. At Earl's garage, they stopped running, turned right and walked toward the south side of town.

He waited until they were out of sight before he felt at ease about the situation. The oldest boy was big and intimidating, but he wasn't about to put up with anybody hassling a little girl.

Cindy looked up at him with her big brown eyes. He was glad to see she wasn't struggling to get a breath any more.

"Thanks for believing me, Mr. Martin."

"Was it true what ya said about yer book?"

"Yeah," she said. "Just ask Shirley."

"No need," he said. "Go on in an' git yerself one of Aunt Maude's cookies."

She darted toward the front door, and when she was safely inside the store, he looked over at the café. Irene was at the front window, smiling at him. He had known her since she was born, but he didn't remember her smiling that much in her whole life.

"Whatever's goin' on must be somethin' good."

Twenty-four

The library's grand opening was a huge success, and two boys from the church choir solved the banner dilemma. They strung it across the ends of the bookcases where it was out of the way but visible from the front door.

Aunt Maude spent most of her time in the kitchen. When the children weren't helping bake cookies, the adults were peeking at the recipe card on the counter. They didn't know the card was a fake and Aunt Maude baked her famous cookies from memory.

Grandma spent most of the day greeting customers and leading tours of the book shelves. Repeatedly, she explained the holding area where their books would be stored until they came to read them again.

I spent the day showing the younger kids my special shelves and helping them choose something to read. For the older kids, I searched through Grandma's books for something they would find interesting. The whole experience was fun, and it reconfirmed my desire to be a teacher.

By the time we closed for the day, all the cookies were eaten, and the holding area was half-filled with Grandma's books. The other half was filled with comics and several classic children's books.

Even though I was exhausted from helping with the grand opening, I woke up early. My mind wouldn't stop thinking about Irene's wedding and all the work I had to do.

There was no sense in lying awake and worrying about it. I got up, made the bed and took my morning shower. After I dressed in shorts, a sleeveless blouse and sandals, I combed my wet hair into the usual ponytail.

When I opened the bedroom door, I didn't hear any sounds coming from downstairs. To keep from waking Grandma and Aunt Maude, I tiptoed down the steps and into the kitchen. I was surprised to find George sitting beside his food bowl.

"Why aren't you in bed, big guy?" I whispered.

He wagged his tail, and stared at me with his big round eyes. There was no way to resist his charm. I filled his food bowl with his breakfast portion of kibble and refilled his water bowl.

"Okay, George," I said. "That should make you feel better."

He gobbled down his kibble, lapped up a little water and spun around and around at my feet. I loved watching his happy dance, but I was afraid his nails clicking against the wood floor would wake Grandma and Aunt Maude.

I picked up my writing tablet and pencil from the counter and walked toward the back door. George stopped spinning and padded along behind me.

When I opened the door, he brushed past me, found his favorite spot in the yard and did his business. By the time I walked outside and over to the swing, he was already there waiting for me.

"You must be in a really big hurry today, big guy."

I tossed the tablet and pencil on the lawn and lifted him onto the swing. The instant his feet hit the seat he started to spin again. The whole swing wobbled until he stopped spinning and collapsed on his end of the seat.

"Done?" I said.

He rested his chin on his front paws and wouldn't look at me. I ignored his snub, picked up the tablet and pencil and sat down on my end of the swing.

"We had a good time yesterday, George," I said. "Too bad you slept through most of it."

He rolled onto his back and sighed. While I rubbed his chest, I leaned against the backrest and closed my eyes. For several minutes, I listened to the creaking of the ropes rubbing against the tree limb.

"It's okay if we take a little nap, big guy," I said. "We're tired."

The writing tablet and pencil were in my lap, but I didn't have the energy to write. I had never stooped or stretched or talked so much in my life as I did at the grand opening.

"Okay, Shirley," I said to myself. "You can't stall forever."

There were only seven days to arrange Irene's wedding, and she was counting on me to pull off a miracle. I couldn't afford the time to sit and rest.

"But where do I begin?"

"How about at the beginning?"

"Jim?"

My eyes flew open, and I sat straight up. He was standing only a few yards away, staring at me.

Instead of his usual jeans and T-shirt, he wore khaki pants, a short-sleeved dress shirt and a new pair of tennis shoes. His wavy blond hair was neatly trimmed, and I didn't see his baseball cap anywhere.

"Are you talking to yourself again?" he said.

I laughed, threw the tablet and pencil on the ground and jumped off the swing. The sudden jolt woke George, and he sat up and yipped.

I picked him up and set him on the ground so he wouldn't fall off the seat. Then, I turned around and ran over to Jim.

"It's about time you got back," I said.

We threw our arms around each other, and I hugged him as hard as I could. Even though it was our first hug, it felt natural and not a bit awkward.

I wanted the hug to go on forever, but George had other plans. He stood at our feet and scratched at our legs until Jim let go of me and picked him up.

"It's okay, George," he said. "I'm home now."

I reached up and scratched the little pug behind his ears. I couldn't be angry with him for interrupting us when he looked at me with his big round eyes.

"How was your interview?"

"I guess it went okay," he said. "You're looking at their newest intern."

"Yes," I said. "I knew you were perfect for the job."

I stretched my arms around him and George and gave them both a big hug. Jim laughed at me, and George licked my face.

"Aunt Maude and your grandma are cooking up a storm in there," he said. "They sent me to get you."

I let go of them and took a step back. I was anxious to hear everything about his trip, but I couldn't keep Grandma and Aunt Maude waiting. If I did, I wouldn't get anything to eat— again.

"I forgot to ask why you're so dressed up this morning, Jim."

"It's kind of a special occasion."

"What do you mean?"

"You'll see soon enough," he said. "Let's go."

He put George on the ground, opened the back door and let the little pug walk inside ahead of us. He led Jim and me all the way through the wide hallway, but when we got to the arched doorway we stopped.

"Is this the special occasion?" I said.

"Yep."

The table was expanded to its full length and covered with Grandma's lace tablecloth. Cindy, Sarah and Mr. Spencer were sitting along one side. Aunt Maude was sitting on the other side next to two empty chairs, and Grandma was seated at the head of the table.

"Hi, everybody," Jim said. "Sorry we kept you waiting."

"We'd never start breakfast without our guest of honor," Aunt Maude said.

Jim and I washed our hands at the sink, walked over to the table and sat down on the empty chairs next to her. I leaned over and whispered to him.

"When did you know about this?"

"Dad told me this morning."

Grandma tapped her spoon against her water glass. When she had everyone's attention, she raised the glass and held it out in front of her.

"Thank you for coming to help us celebrate Jimmy's new job."

"Here, here," Mr. Spencer said and lifted his glass of water. "A toast to my son."

We all raised our water glasses and looked at Jim. With all our attention on him, his face turned bright red.

"Thank you," he said and drank a sip from his glass.

Always the perfect hostess, Grandma picked up a platter of Aunt Maude's waffles and another of her crispy bacon. She passed them around the table, and we all took huge helpings of everything.

While we ate, everyone talked at once, and it was impossible for me to follow all the conversations. I finally gave up the effort and ate my food until Grandma tapped her spoon on her water glass again.

"It's been lovely having all of you here for breakfast," she said. "Now, it's time to go to work."

We all took the hint, cleared the table and hauled everything to the sink. When the tablecloth was refolded and the table leaf was stored in the pantry again, all the company left except Jim.

I started to walk him to the front door, but before we were half-way there, he grabbed my hand. He pulled me into the aisle between two bookcases where it was private and out of Grandma's line of sight.

"I really had a good time this morning," he said.

"Me, too."

He put his hands on my shoulders and pulled me close. When I looked up at him, he leaned down and gave me a quick, gentle kiss.

"Shirley?"

"Huh?"

"I forgot to bring the souvenirs I bought for you."

His kiss left my heart racing, and I couldn't put two coherent words together. The last thing on my mind was souvenirs.

"I'll bring them with me next time, okay?"

"Okay."

He took his hands from my shoulders, and we walked hand in hand to the front door. My heart was still racing, and I could barely feel the floor under my feet.

"How about a picnic lunch?" he said.

"Okay."

"Pick you up at one o'clock?"

"Okay."

He let go of my hand, opened the door and walked out to his father's truck. I stood in the doorway and watched Mr. Spencer back his truck out of the parking space and drive up the street.

I didn't move until the truck turned onto the side road and drove in the direction of the mill. When it went out of sight, I closed the door, leaned my back against it and took a deep breath.

I looked over at the kitchen and saw Grandma and Aunt Maude at the sink, watching me. When they smiled, I knew it wouldn't be long before everybody in Willowdale knew how Jim and I felt about each other.

Twenty-five

After I helped Aunt Maude wash and dry the breakfast dishes, I helped Grandma straightened up the library. One by one, I fit the old books from the attic into their proper places and dusted the shelves. It took longer than I thought it would, and I had to rush to make the picnic sandwiches.

Once they were wrapped and in the refrigerator, I scribbled a list of wedding plans on a sheet of paper. I folded it, put it in my blouse pocket and walked across the street to the café.

Instead of going in through the front door, I sneaked in through the back. Just as I hoped, Miss Carter was in the dining room talking to a customer with her back turned toward me.

To avoid her and her usual condescending attitude, I darted into the kitchen before she turned around. I was in a good mood, and I didn't want to give her the opportunity to spoil it.

Irene was at the griddle, flipping hamburgers for the lunch crowd. On the counter beside the griddle were plates with buttered buns waiting to be filled.

I watched her scoop up a burger with her spatula, set it on a bun and pile lettuce and a tomato on top. She slipped the finished hamburger onto a plate and added a handful of potato chips. When she slid the plate onto the service window shelf, she slapped a bell on the counter.

"Burger up."

I tiptoed over to her and spoke just above a whisper. I was prepared to duck down behind the counter if necessary to avoid being seen by Miss Carter.

"Good morning," I said.

Irene turned around and wiped her hands on her apron. Her clothes reeked with the smell of grease, and I was glad she didn't give me one of her welcoming hugs.

"Mornin', Shirley," she said. "Why're you whisperin'?"

"I don't want to deal with your boss today," I said.

"Why's that?"

I looked through the service window to see where Miss Carter was. Fortunately, she was busing a table toward the front of the dining room and couldn't hear me.

"Because," I said. "Jim and I are going on our first date."

"You and Jim?"

"Don't look so surprised," I said. "We get along just fine now."

"If you say so," she said. "Where's he takin' you?"

"On a picnic."

She nodded, turned toward the griddle and flipped over two more burgers. When she looked at me again, she wiped rivulets of perspiration from her face with the hem of her apron.

"When're you goin'?"

"He's picking me up in a couple of minutes, but I wanted to drop this off first."

I pulled the folded sheet of paper from my blouse pocket and laid it on the counter. I wanted to get her input on a few of the things I wrote down.

"What is it?"

"Your wedding plans," I said. "When you get a chance, look it over and let me know what you think."

"Don't have to," she said. "I trust you."

I wasn't very comfortable with that. A bride should have the last say in the planning, but I picked up the paper and put it back in my pocket.

"I'd better go," I said. "Talk to you soon."

Irene threw me a quick wave. Then, she turned around and flipped over the rest of the burgers.

I was about to leave the kitchen until I saw Miss Carter on the wall phone beside the service window. The plate with the hamburger was still on the shelf, and all my café training rushed back to me.

Grandma would never have allowed me to leave an order on the shelf and let the food get cold. It took all my will power to keep from grabbing the plate and serving it to the customer myself.

Instead, I hid behind the kitchen wall before Miss Carter saw me and waited for the opportunity to sneak away. I planned to leave while she was busy with the call until I overheard her side of the conversation.

"I have a week before the opening," she said, "and I intend to hire only the most competent help for my bed and breakfast."

There was a long pause in her conversation. I could have left right then, but the temptation to stay was too great. I wanted to hear more about her hiring people to work at Grandma's old farmhouse.

"No," she said. "If I want to earn the trust of these people, I need to hire locally."

The clock on the wall in the dining room chimed once. Jim was probably at the store, waiting for me. Thank goodness I already made our sandwiches.

I pressed my back against the wall and eased closer to the kitchen door. It was the perfect time to leave, but Miss Carter wasn't done talking.

"I will retain Irene at the café, of course," she said. "She is a much better cook than you find in most restaurants."

I couldn't disagree with that. Mom and I didn't eat out enough to compare Irene's cooking to a restaurant's, but I really liked her cooking.

"Mr. Martin will continue on as my handyman at the café," she said. "He's old and moves too slowly, but he does alright."

If Irene and Mr. Martin were staying at the café, who else could she find? Willowdale wasn't like my home town of South Bend. There weren't a lot of people to choose from.

"I'll primarily work from the café," she said. "I wouldn't dare trust an employee with the cash register."

There was another long pause. I really needed to leave and meet Jim, but I wanted to hear everything she had to say.

"Yes, I'll definitely need a live-in manager at the farmhouse," she said. "Whoever it is will also prepare breakfast for my quests."

She hung up the phone and walked away from the counter without taking the plate of food. From where I stood, I couldn't see which direction she went.

I slid my back along the wall a little farther and peeked around the door frame. She was standing at the register, counting out change for a man in a business suit. While she was distracted, I escaped from the kitchen and ran out the back door.

Twenty-six

I ran around the side of the café, past the patio fence and across the street between traffic. Mr. Spencer's truck was parked in front of the General Store.

Being late for a date was rude, but being late for a first date was inexcusable. I hated to think what Jim thought about me right then.

When I pushed the door open, he was sitting on one of the sofas, explaining his internship to Grandma and Aunt Maude. He had changed out of his good clothes and into his usual jeans and T-shirt.

"I'll only be a gofer at first," he said. "I should learn a lot about architecture by running errands."

"You absolutely should," Aunt Maude said.

"I have to wear slacks and a dress shirt," he said, "but I don't have to wear a tie."

"Ties can be so cumbersome," Grandma said.

Nobody seemed to notice me standing at the front door. All the attention was focused on Jim.

"Hi, everybody," I said. "I got stuck at the café."

"That's fine, dear," Grandma said with a wave of her hand. "Jimmy has kept us entertained."

I closed the door, walked over to the sofas and plopped down next to Jim. Aunt Maude kicked off her slippers and put her bare feet up on the coffee table. Her ankles were swollen more than usual.

"Hey, Shirley," Jim said. "What do you mean by stuck?"

I wiggled a little on the cushion in order to get more comfortable and took a deep breath. There was no way to explain other than to tell the truth, so I blurted it out.

"I was eavesdropping."

Jim smiled a little, but Grandma didn't. She crossed her arms in front of her chest and stared at me.

"You'll have to do a better job of explaining yourself than that," she said.

"Miss Carter was on the phone, and I stayed to listen."

I wasn't helping my case any, but I didn't care. What I heard could potentially change the lives of a lot of people in town.

Aunt Maude dropped her feet to the floor and put her slippers back on. She sat up straight and scooted to the edge of the sofa.

"Go ahead, Shirley," she said. "I want to know what you heard."

Grandma unfolded her arms, picked up her coffee cup and took a sip. When she put the cup down, she was smiling.

"Oh, alright, young lady," she said. "What did you hear?"

I explained Miss Carter's plan to hire more help. I thought all of them would be interested, but I was wrong.

"So what?" Jim said. "It's her business."

"Don't you see?" I said. "She'll need someone to live at the farmhouse to cook and manage it when she's not there."

"Yeah, so?"

"I know the exact person she should hire."

Grandma and Aunt Maude sat up even straighter and stared at me. I had their full attention at last.

"Well, of all things," Grandma said. "Tell us who you have in mind?"

"Sarah."

I didn't know if Sarah would be interested in the job. What I did know was she and Cindy deserved to live in a real house. Not in a backroom without a kitchen or a proper bathroom.

Grandma picked up her coffee cup and took several more sips. When she put the cup back down on the coffee table, she nodded at me.

"The idea has merit," she said "We must investigate the possibility immediately."

"Thank you, Grandma," I said, "but what do you mean by immediately?"

"I mean right this minute."

She pushed herself up from the sofa, picked up her cup and hurried to the kitchen. Jim, Aunt Maude and I looked back and forth at one another.

"What just happened?" I said.

"Looks like our picnic's postponed," Jim said.

I glanced over at him and shook my head. Postponing our date was not what I had in mind. I was just worried about Sarah and Cindy.

"Once your grandma gets a notion," Aunt Maude said, "there's no stopping her."

Jim jumped up from the sofa and ran his fingers through his hair. It was what he always did when he was stalling for time. When he dropped his hand to his side, he looked at me.

"What should we do first?" he said.

Before I could think of an answer, Grandma came back to the sitting area. She tucked loose strands of hair into the bun at her neck and a clean hankie under her belt.

"The first thing we do," she said, "is speak to Sarah."

"Right now?" I said.

"Right now."

"What if she has customers?"

"Ye gods, Shirley," Grandma said. "The customers can wait."

When I stood up, she took me by the elbow and steered me toward the front of the store. I opened the door for her and looked back over my shoulder.

Aunt Maude was right behind us in her mule slippers, and Jim was behind her with George tucked under his arm. When we were all outside, Jim closed the door, locked it and hid the key above the door frame.

Like a general leading her troops, Grandma marched us up the sidewalk and across the street to Kut and Kurl. I was excited for Sarah, but I felt sorry for her at the same time. We looked more like an invasion than four friends and a pug going for a visit.

When we walked into the beauty shop, there were two customers sitting under hair dryers. Sarah was across the room at one of the sinks, washing a woman's hair.

Jim, George, Aunt Maude and I stopped just inside the door, but Grandma didn't pause. She went directly over to Sarah and stood beside the sink.

"Sarah," she said.

"Is something wrong, Mrs. Ivey?"

She finished rinsing the woman's hair and wrapped a towel around her head. The woman stood up, walked over to one of the swivel chairs and sat down.

"I was here first, Mrs. Ivey," she said. "You have to wait your turn."

"Nonsense," Grandma said. "It's imperative I speak to Sarah at once."

"Is it Cindy?" Sarah said. "Has something happened?"

Instead of answering her, Grandma turned around, pushed past all of us and walked out the door. Sarah looked worried and confused, and she didn't hesitate to follow us outside.

"Let's sit down, shall we?" Grandma said.

She and Aunt Maude sat on the bench in front of the store, and Sarah sat down next to them. Jim and I sat on the curb with our feet in the street, and George curled up in Jim's lap.

"Is Cindy alright?" Sarah said.

"I haven't seen your daughter since breakfast," Grandma said. "We're here about another matter."

"What is it?"

"Elaine Carter is hiring staff for her bed and breakfast, and we feel you would be a perfect candidate."

"I already have a job."

"Yes, you are a wonderful hairdresser, but this is an opportunity you really must consider."

"What kind of a job is it?"

Grandma paused, and I twisted around to look at her. She looked down at me, and grinned.

"My granddaughter will explain," she said.

I got up and stood in front of Sarah. I knew from Jim's experience Miss Carter was an extremely demanding employer. I hoped Sarah was up to the challenge.

"Miss Carter needs a live-in manager and cook at her new bed and breakfast," I said. "The job starts in a week."

Sarah's mouth dropped open, and her face turned pale. Had she already heard about Miss Carter's reputation?

"I'm sorry," she said. "I'm the wrong person for the job."

"This would be perfect for you and Cindy," I said. "You'd live in a beautiful house, and you'd only have to cook breakfast."

"I can't," she said.

"Why?"

"Because I don't know anything about keeping books, and I'm an awful cook."

"Oh."

Grandma got up and paced back and forth in front of the bench. After a few seconds, she stopped and looked down at Sarah.

"I have a solution," she said. "I know how to keep books, and Maude is a very good cook."

"You're not thinking what I think you're thinking, are you?" I said.

"I am," Grandma said. "I believe Maude and I are more than qualified to teach Sarah everything she'll need to know."

"Marie and I can start your lessons today," Aunt Maude said. "Right after you close up the shop."

"That's too much to ask."

"You're not asking," Grandma said. "We're volunteering."

"Besides," I said. "They never take no for an answer."

"How can I learn everything in only a week?"

Grandma stood as tall as she could and tilted her chin up. When she spoke, I knew the matter was settled.

"Never underestimate your own strength, Sarah, and the determination of the Ivey and Ellis women."

Twenty-seven

Watching Aunt Maude teach Sarah to cook a proper breakfast was fascinating. She covered every tiny detail of the process, and I marveled at her patience.

The store smelled like charred bacon and burned toast, but nothing went to waste. Cindy, Jim and I sat at the table, tearing off the best parts of the bacon and scraping black off the toast.

The three of us called ourselves the guinea pigs, and that was alright with me. We were having a feast on the scraps of Sarah's mistakes.

"Will I ever get this right?" she said.

"This is only your first lesson," Aunt Maude said. "Tomorrow, we'll start your next lesson before the library opens."

Sarah's face was pink from standing over the stove, and her bib apron was smeared with grease. I felt sorry for her, but I didn't want to say anything in front of her daughter.

"This is fun, Mama," Cindy said. "Can we be your guinea pigs again tomorrow?"

Sarah looked up from the frying pan and glared at her daughter. I could almost read her mind, but I gave her credit for not saying what she was thinking.

"Your mother's working really hard," Jim said. "Why don't we go do something else for a while?"

"Like what?"

"Well," he said. "We could go for a ride."

"Really?"

"If your mother says it's okay."

"Mama?"

Before Sarah answered, a shaft of smoke rose from the frying pan, and she grabbed a pot holder from the counter. While she moved the pan off the burner, a cloud of smoke billowed from the toaster. She unplugged it, grabbed the blackened pieces of toast and threw them in the sink.

"I'll open the door, Jim," I said. "You turn on the fan."

We both jumped up from the table. I ran to the front door and pulled it wide open. Jim leaned over the stove and released the chain on the ventilation fan.

"I'm so sorry," Sarah said.

She plopped down on a kitchen chair, propped her elbows on the table and covered her face with her hands. When I saw her shoulders shake, I wanted to cry along with her.

"A ride would be okay," Aunt Maude said. "Isn't that right, Sarah?"

She put a hand on her shoulder, but Sarah never looked up or said a word. She kept her face covered and nodded.

"Okay, Cindy," Jim said. "There's a place I think you'll really like."

Cindy got up, walked around the table and stared at her mother. When Sarah didn't say anything, I took Cindy's hand

and led her to the door. Jim followed behind us, and I heard Grandma's voice as we walked out the door.

"I believe that is quite enough cooking for one afternoon," she said.

I stopped just outside the door and let go of Cindy's hand. When she looked up at me, there were tears in her eyes.

"Your mother's fine," I said. "She's just a little tired."

"Really?"

"Really."

Jim climbed into his father's truck and started the engine. I knew there was nothing I could do to help Sarah, but there was something I could do for Cindy.

"Go ahead and get in the truck," I said. "Tell Jim I'll be right there."

I hurried into the store, walked past Sarah and Aunt Maude and opened the refrigerator. I gathered all but three of the peanut butter and jelly sandwiches I made and set them on the counter. Then, I picked out six red apples and three bottles of pop.

"There's no reason we can't have a little picnic along the way," I said to them. "There are more sandwiches in the refrigerator in case you get hungry."

Sarah was still sitting at the table, and she looked up at me with red-rimmed eyes. I wanted to reassure her everything would be alright, but I wasn't positive about that. If cooking was a challenge for her, how would she do at keeping books?

I went to the pantry and found the wicker picnic basket. Grandma came in and picked up the cookie container from one of the top shelves.

"Don't worry about Sarah, dear," she said. "We'll discover where she excels and build upon that."

"You would have made a great teacher, Grandma."

I left her in the pantry rearranging shelves and carried the basket to the kitchen. While I filled it with the picnic supplies, Sarah stood at the sink and washed dirty pans and dishes.

"Thanks for taking Cindy with you."

"Of course, Sarah," I said. "We won't be late."

I picked up the basket and walked out to Mr. Spencer's truck. After I put the basket in the back, I climbed into the cab and rolled down the window.

"All set?" Jim said.

"All set," Cindy and I said together.

He drove to the end of Main Street and turned onto the gravel road leading to his father's mill. I didn't know where we were going, and I didn't care. We all needed a break before Sarah had her next lesson.

Twenty-eight

I put George on the swing and sat down next to him. By the time I opened my tablet to start writing, he was already asleep.

"I know," I said to him. "Watching me write my daily letter to Dad must be pretty boring."

Of course, I never mailed the letters. They were my way of keeping a daily journal, and nobody else ever read them. To make sure of that, I hid them in a manila envelope in the bottom draw of my desk.

"Let's see, big guy, where do I begin?"

I tucked my left leg up under me and kicked the swing into motion with my right foot. When the creaking of the ropes began, I closed my eyes and listened.

"Maybe I should start with a nap."

It seemed I was destined to be exhausted. Working most of the day at the library's grand opening had been physically demanding. Constantly climbing up and down the wooden ladder to reach books on the top shelves was more exercise than I expected.

"Today should be better," I said. "Everybody who came on Thursday knows about Grandma's storage shelf and how the books are arranged."

Before I was lulled to sleep by the gentle back and forth motion of the swing, I heard a click. Only one thing I knew made that sound, and that was the latch on the gate.

I opened my eyes and looked over toward the corner of the fence. The gate slowly swung open an inch at a time. I couldn't imagine who would sneak into the yard until I saw the hem of the floral sundress.

"Come on in, Cindy," I said.

"You sure?"

"Yes, I'm sure."

"Is it okay if I come see George?"

"He'd like that."

I wasn't in the mood for a visitor, but I couldn't turn Cindy away. I was getting used to her following me around, and I thought she should have a place where she felt welcome.

She walked across the lawn and stopped in front of the swing. Her smile turned into a frown when she saw George sleeping.

"I better come back later."

"No, that's okay," I said. "He can sleep in your lap as well as on the seat."

I stopped the swing, tossed the tablet and pencil on the ground and lifted George out of her way. She climbed onto the seat, scooted all the way back against the backrest and stretched her legs out in front of her. When I placed the little pug on her lap, George lifted his head.

"Hi, George," she said.

He opened his eyes halfway and snorted once. Then, he closed his eyes and went back to sleep.

Cindy ran her hand down his back and smiled. It looked as though he had the same effect on her as he did on me. I always felt more relaxed when I was with him.

"Thanks for the comic book, Shirley."

"I'm glad you like it, but you'll have to read the rest of them in the library."

"Why?"

"Grandma doesn't lend them or any of her books," I said. "She has a place to keep them if you don't finish reading during library hours."

"Yeah, I know."

"From now on, the library's only open on Wednesdays and Saturdays."

"Okay."

We sat for several minutes without speaking. All the while, Cindy ran her hand down George's back, and I pumped the swing with my foot.

"Your mother's having another cooking lesson," I finally said.

"Yeah."

"Don't you want to go watch?"

"No," she said. "I want to stay with George."

Again, we sat without speaking. A light breeze ruffled the wisps of hair around my face, but my ponytail felt heavy against my back.

Sarah said she could fix my hair in a new style. Maybe it was time for a change. That would really surprise Mom and all my friends.

"Shirley?"

"Yes."

"Is it okay if I come and sit on the swing if you're not here?"

I looked down at her and George. They looked content with each other, and I was almost jealous. It was a ridiculous reaction, but there it was.

"You'll have to ask my grandma or Aunt Maude," I said. "It's their place."

"Okay."

There was no reason she shouldn't enjoy the swing. I was leaving in a week, and I wouldn't be back to spend another summer. Besides, George would love her company.

I was about to tell her that, but I didn't get the chance. The back door flew open, and Aunt Maude stuck her head outside. She was dressed in an old housedress and her mule slippers. Instead of a braid across the top of her head, her hair hung straight down to her shoulders.

"Time for breakfast, you two."

"Are we having burned toast again?" Cindy said.

Aunt Maude laughed, but didn't say anything else. She closed the door behind her, and Cindy looked up at me.

"Maybe burned bacon?"

"I don't know, but we'd better hurry," I said. "Grandma and Aunt Maude won't keep breakfast for us for very long."

I took George from her, set him on the lawn and picked up my tablet and pencil. Cindy jumped down from the swing and followed George and me into the store.

I smelled French toast all the way from the back door, and it didn't smell burned. When my stomach let out a loud growl, Cindy looked up at me and laughed.

"I'm hungry, too," she said.

"If you think Aunt Maude's pancakes were great," I said. "Wait 'til you taste her French toast."

Cindy practically sprinted to the kitchen, leaving George and me behind. I heard a chair scrape against the floor, and within a second or two, I heard Grandma's voice.

"Oh, no, young lady," she said. "Everyone in this house washes their hands before sitting down to eat."

"You listen to Mrs. Ivey," Sarah said.

"Yes, Mama."

By the time George and I got to the kitchen, Cindy was at the sink, washing her hands. I laid my tablet and pencil on the counter and joined her.

"Take your time," I said. "You don't want Grandma to send you back here to wash again."

"She'd do that?"

"You can count on it."

She scrubbed even harder and worked up more lather than necessary. After she rinsed all the soap from her hands, I finished drying mine and gave her the towel.

When her hands were dry, I threw the towel on the counter and sat down. Cindy sat next to me, and Sarah and Aunt

Maude sat across from us. As usual, Grandma sat at the head of the table.

"Good morning, everyone," Sarah said. "This is my first official bed and breakfast—breakfast."

I was amazed to see what she learned since her disastrous lesson the day before. French toast was stacked on a platter in the center of the table, and a bowl of scrambled eggs was beside it. Next to each proper place setting was a small glass of orange juice.

"Mama," Cindy said. "You can cook."

We all laughed at her, but she was right. Sarah's transformation into a cook in just a single day was miraculous.

"When you're done eating, Cindy," Aunt Maude said, "I'd like you to take George for a walk."

Cindy's mouth fell open, and mine did, too. Everybody knew walking George was a special honor, and Aunt Maude didn't trust him with just anyone.

"Can I?" she said.

"If you want to."

"I do, I do."

"Then you better eat," Grandma said. "We haven't much time before the library opens."

The little jealousy demon whispered in my ear again, but I chose to ignore it. Aunt Maude needed someone to walk George when I wasn't there. It only made sense to pick a person who loved George and was old enough to handle the responsibility.

"Everyone, help yourselves," Sarah said.

When the food was passed around the table, I took two pieces of French toast and a heaping spoonful of eggs. I waited until everyone was busy eating before I leaned my head close to Grandma's ear and whispered to her.

"How did Aunt Maude do it?"

"She started with the foods Sarah wanted to cook," she said, "and expanded the menu from there."

"What about keeping the books?"

"I spent some time with her while you and Jimmy took Cindy for a ride yesterday," she said.

"How did she do?"

"She is gifted with figures," Grandma said. "I think she would make an excellent bookkeeper."

I sat back up and took a big bite of the eggs. They almost melted in my mouth, and I nodded at Grandma.

"These are the best eggs I've ever eaten."

Grandma smiled at me and winked. In just one day, she and Aunt Maude had taught me a life-long lesson about teaching. Each student has his own strengths and learns in his own way, and they took the time to discover what those were for Sarah.

"Can we have eggs every day, Mama?" Cindy said.

"Maybe not every day."

Grandma always bragged my scrambled eggs were the best this side of the Mississippi River. I lost that title to Sarah with her very first meal.

Twenty-nine

Elaine sat at the front table and looked out across the empty dining room. With no bus scheduled to stop on Saturday, the only customer was Clyde Wilson. As usual, he sat at the counter, sipping coffee and watching Irene at work in the kitchen.

"As long as Irene continues to do her best," she said under her breath, "I won't interfere."

She spun in her chair and looked out the front window. The only action appeared to be across the street. Several cars were parked in front of the General Store, and people of all ages walked in and out of the door.

"I never imagined a library would be so popular."

She looked up at the sign Mr. Spencer made for the store and secretly admitted it was the perfect finishing touch. The background was stained a medium brown, and the routed letters were painted a muted shade of red. The combination gave the store a welcoming, down-home feel.

"Appropriate for two old women," she said, "but my sign evokes the feel of youth and vitality."

She spun back around and picked up the pencil in front of her. She opened the tablet on the table to the first page and drew a line down the center of it. Above the left column she wrote Elaine's, and above the right column she wrote Elaine's Bed and Breakfast.

Filling in the column on the left was easy. There were only three names to list. The first was Irene as the cook, and the second was Mr. Martin as the handyman. The third was her own as the hostess, waitress, cashier and gift shop entrepreneur.

The column on the right was even easier to fill. There weren't any names to list except her own as proprietress.

"I assured Mr. Daily at the bank I would hire local talent," she said to herself, "but what am I to do at this late date?"

The bed and breakfast was scheduled to open in one week, and not hiring staff was the height of incompetence. If she were an employee and not the boss, she would have already been fired because of it.

Irene was a wonderful cook, but she couldn't be expected to work at both locations. Besides, she needed the girl to stay in town and keep her informed of business developments.

Mr. Martin was diligent about his job, but he was no longer a young man. He simply wouldn't have the endurance to work at both the café and the farmhouse.

Physically, it would be impossible for her to hostess the farmhouse and the café at the same time. Finding a competent manager and cook for the bed and breakfast might be more difficult than she anticipated.

"I haven't the luxury of wallowing in self-pity about this," she whispered. "I must begin immediately to scour the county for qualified people."

She stood up, turned around and glared out the window at Marie and Maude's store. She had hoped their retirement would mean less competition for her, but the town's loyalty to old friends was unshakeable.

"What do I have to do to earn respect in this town?"

Everyone liked Irene and Mr. Martin. She thought their presence would attract all their friends to the café.

"Obviously, that didn't work," she said. "Perhaps the article and the coupons in tomorrow's paper will."

She glanced at the copies of Saturday's newspaper in the rack by the front door. The Sunday edition would be delivered directly to the homes around the county.

"By Monday morning, I'm confident my café will be overflowing with customers," she said. "Who can resist a discount on a meal?"

Thirty

The glow-in-the-dark hands on my alarm clock read three o'clock in the morning. Even though the little gable window was wide open, it was too warm in my room to sleep. I got up, tiptoed over to the window and looked out at the back yard.

It was a moonless night, and everything in the yard blended into shades of black and grey. I could barely make out a silhouette of the swing.

Grandpa and I had spent hours sitting on it, counting cars on the county road beyond the farmhouse. I missed those times we spent together, but I had more important things to do than reminisce.

The sheet of paper with Irene's wedding plans was on the built-in seat. It was too dark to read, but I didn't want to turn on a light. Instead, I mentally visualized everything left on the list to complete.

Although the wedding ceremony was only for close friends and invited guests, the reception was open to everyone. It was the biggest item left to tackle, and I needed help. I had to find someone to announce it to the town and organize the food.

"Think," I said to myself. "You're running out of time."

Miss Spitz manned the telephone switchboard on Sundays, and everybody knew she loved to gossip. I couldn't think of a better person to spread the word about the reception.

"After breakfast, I'll get her on the phone."

With that decided I wandered over to the closet, put a long-sleeved blouse over my nightgown and slipped into my moccasins. Since I couldn't sleep anyway, I decided to go downstairs and find a good book to read.

I picked up the flashlight from the nightstand and clicked it on. The batteries were weak and the beam was yellow, but it would do.

When I was half-way down the stairs, I heard a knock on the front door. I stopped, turned off the flashlight and listened for more sounds.

"Who'd come here in the middle of the night?" I whispered to myself.

I was worried for the four of us, and imagined all kinds of scenarios. The one that made the least sense was a burglar. He wouldn't knock on the door before breaking in and robbing the place.

There were three more knocks, and then a long stretch of silence. I waited and hoped whoever it was went away, but the knocking started again.

"Okay," I said. "Somebody has to answer the door."

When I didn't hear Grandma or Aunt Maude get up, I knew that somebody was me. If I didn't answer it, whoever it was might never stop knocking.

At the bottom of the stairs, I walked toward the front of the room, waving my arms in front of me. When I finally got to the door, I eased it open a crack and blocked it with my foot. If I had to, I was prepared to slam the door shut and run to the phone for help.

"Hey, Shirley."

When I saw Jim outside, I pulled the door all the way open. I didn't know why he was there, but I wasn't dressed for company.

He was dressed as he usually was in jeans and a T-shirt. His curly blond hair was covered by his old baseball cap.

"Jim Spencer," I said. "What are you doing here?"

He grinned, pulled off his cap and slapped it against his pant leg. Bits of grain and chaff fell onto the sidewalk.

"Go get dressed," he said, "and do something about your hair."

Who did he think he was, ordering me around? It was the middle of the night, and I wasn't in the mood to deal with his attitude.

"Why would I do that?"

"Because there's something I want you to see" he said. "If you don't hurry, you'll miss the whole thing."

"What thing?"

"Stop asking questions and get going."

I frowned at him and hesitated for a second or two. He made whatever it was sound urgent, and I couldn't help but be curious.

"Okay," I said, "but this better be good."

With the help of the flashlight, I hurried upstairs and changed into a pair of shorts and a sleeveless blouse. I kicked off my moccasins and exchanged them for socks and tennis shoes.

I gathered my hair at the back of my neck and secured it with a rubber band. I couldn't see a clear reflection of myself in the mirror above the dresser. I just had to trust I looked okay.

When I got back downstairs, the front door was still wide open, but Jim was gone. Outside, a truck engine was running, and I was afraid he was leaving without me.

"I'm coming," I said under my breath.

I turned off the flashlight, set it on the floor and snatched a sweater from a hook beside the door. I stepped outside and eased the door closed behind me.

It was pitch black out, and Jim snapped on the truck's headlights for me. I managed to reach the truck and climb inside without hurting myself, but the floor of the cab was littered with paper.

"What's all this?" I said.

"Your Grandma's posters," he said. "I took them down for her, but I haven't had a chance to throw them away."

"Oh, no," I said. "I completely forgot to leave Grandma a note."

"That's okay."

"I can't just leave without telling her where I'm going."

"Don't worry so much," he said. "It'll be fine."

"That's easy for you to say."

When he pulled the truck away from the curb, it became the second time in my life I sneaked out at night. Both times were with Jim, but this time, I didn't know where we were going. I assumed it wasn't to paint the water tower again.

"Where are we headed?" I said.

"You'll see."

He turned his head and showed off his wide, toothy smile for me. It didn't make me feel any better. I was at his mercy, and I wasn't sure I liked that idea.

Thirty-one

Jim drove around the countryside in a zigzag pattern until I was completely disoriented. Without moonlight, I couldn't see which way we went or what roads we were on.

"Are we lost?"

"We're not lost," he said. "We're here."

When he slowed the truck and pulled into the driveway, I knew exactly where we were. At night, the place felt eerie. There were no lights on in the farmhouse, and Sebastian wasn't there to greet us.

"Does Mr. Wilson know we're coming?"

"I think so."

I didn't expect Jim to explain, so I sat quietly and waited to see what would happen next. I didn't have to wait long.

He eased the truck across the barnyard, past the dilapidated outbuildings and onto the narrow dirt track leading to the pond. The truck was wider than Grandpa's, and Jim had to squeeze it between the wire fence and the small creek.

When we reached the end of the track, Clyde's truck was parked in front of the stand of birch trees. Jim parked right next to it, switched off the headlights and turned off the engine.

"What's going on?" I said.

Without a word, Jim grabbed a flashlight from under the seat, clicked it on and jumped out of the cab. After he slammed the door shut, he ran to the back of the truck. I stayed where I was and watched him through the back window.

He grabbed a blanket and a picnic basket from the bed and carried them over to me. I rolled down the window and stared at the basket.

"A picnic?"

"I owed you one," he said. "Let's go."

I rolled up the window and wrapped the sweater around my shoulders. By the time I climbed out of the truck, Jim was already on the footpath leading to the pond. I followed the beam of his flashlight and ran to catch up to him.

"Don't leave me out here by myself," I said.

In the daylight, following the winding footpath through the woods was a peaceful experience. In the dark, the paper birch trees looked like ghosts with their white, shaggy bark. The thought sent a chill through me.

After several minutes, we came to the end of the birch trees and walked onto the sandy beach beside Mr. Wilson's pond. Irene and Clyde were lying on a blanket next to the water.

"Hi, you two," Irene said.

"Are we late?" Jim said.

"Nope. It's just gettin' good."

I didn't have any idea what she was talking about. She might as well have been speaking another language, and none of them offered an explanation.

"Here," Jim said and handed me the blanket.

"What do you want me to do with this?"

"Put it next to theirs."

I spread the blanket on the sand next to Irene and Clyde, and Jim set the basket down between the blankets. He clicked off the flashlight, flopped flat on his back on the blanket and looked up at the sky.

"There they are," he said.

"Who?"

"If you get down here, you can see for yourself."

Irene giggled a little, but I ignored her and sat down. When I followed Jim's gaze I saw why he was looking at the sky. I learned about meteor showers in science class at school, but I had never seen one before.

I swallowed my embarrassment, kicked off my shoes and peeled off my socks. I stretched out on the blanket with my hands folded under my head and watched the light show.

"Wow."

"Not bad for a first date, huh?" he said.

"Is that what this is?"

"What else?"

I was completely enthralled by the white lines streaking across the sky, one right after the other. There were so many, it looked as though all the stars were falling.

Of course, they weren't. The stars were still in their proper places, and the Milky Way still stretched across the sky.

"Anybody hungry?" Clyde said.

"Go ahead," Jim said. "Help yourself."

I didn't mind sharing our first date. If Jim were more comfortable with that, Irene and Clyde was the couple I would have chosen, too.

"What food did you pack, Jim?" I said.

"I didn't have to pack anything," he said. "Aunt Maude fixed everything for us."

At first I thought I heard wrong. If I didn't and Aunt Maude packed the basket, Grandma had to be right in the middle of it all.

"Grandma knows where we are?"

"Who do you think told me about the meteor shower?"

It was no wonder Grandma and Aunt Maude didn't answer the door when Jim knocked. They planned for me to do it all along. I didn't know if I should laugh or be angry.

While I thought about it, Jim sat up and opened the basket. He handed me an egg salad sandwich and a bottle of pop.

"Didn't Grandma and Aunt Maude want to come see the meteors, too?"

Jim took a huge bite of his sandwich and washed it down with some pop. He was stalling for time, and I knew it.

"They said they've seen them before, but—"

"But what?"

"Your grandma wouldn't allow me to bring you here unless Irene and Clyde came with us."

That explained the double date. If she couldn't be there to act as chaperone, she'd make sure somebody else was.

"Does your dad know we're here, too, Clyde?"

"Yeah."

"Anybody else?"

"Probably everybody else."

I looked up at the meteors one last time. They were impressive, but the idea of being fooled by everyone in town made me sick to my stomach.

"So, everybody knew the plan except me."

"Yeah," Jim said "I thought you'd get a real kick out it."

Well, he thought wrong. I worked in Willowdale for two summers, and I thought everyone accepted me as one of their own. I never expected to be the object of an elaborate joke.

"I'm tired, Jim."

I stood up and tossed my uneaten sandwich and unopened pop back inside the basket. I thrust my arms into the sleeves of my sweater and glared at him.

"Are you okay?" he said.

"No. Take me back to the store."

"What?"

"I have a lot of work to do for the wedding," I said. "I need to get at least a little sleep."

Just because I was angry, it didn't relieve me of my obligation to Clyde and Irene. I'd still make sure they had the wedding of their dreams.

"You sure you have to leave?" Irene said.

"I'm sure."

Jim jumped up and threw his empty waxed paper and pop bottle into the picnic basket. While I put my shoes and socks back on, he picked up the blanket and shook off the sand.

"You two keep the food," he said. "Get the basket back to Mrs. Ivey when you're done."

"Sure thing," Clyde said.

I didn't say goodbye or wait for Jim to lead me back to the truck. I slogged through the sand and started up the footpath alone and in the dark.

The trees still looked spooky, but I forced myself to ignore them. I wanted to get back to the store, finish the wedding plans and go back home where I belonged.

"Don't worry, Jim" I said over my shoulder. "You've satisfied your picnic date obligation."

Neither of us spoke on the ride back to town. I sat close to the passenger door and stared out the side window. Jim looked straight ahead and drove without zigzagging through the countryside.

By the time we reached Willowdale, it was six o'clock and the sky was getting light. The street lights were still on, but there weren't any other cars or trucks on Main Street.

He stopped his dad's truck in front of the store, and I leaped out as if the cab were on fire. I wanted to get upstairs to my room and hide until my train left for South Bend. Of course, that was a ridiculous idea. I had a lot to do before then.

"See you later?" Jim said.

"I don't think so."

I opened the store's front door, eased it closed and stood just inside. I wasn't ready to talk about the trick everyone played on me or the date with Jim, but I didn't need to worry.

All the globe lights in the library were on, and Grandma was in her robe and slippers rearranging books on the shelves. She was too absorbed in her work to notice me.

I didn't see Aunt Maude, but the television in her apartment was turned on. I knew she wouldn't surface until the news program she was watching was over.

Instead of going directly upstairs, I tiptoed over to George and knelt beside him. I rested my hand on his back, and when he opened his eyes, I whispered to him.

"Hi, big guy."

When he looked at me and wagged his tail, I couldn't help but smile. That moment with him was the one bright light in a very early morning filled with disappointment.

Thirty-two

I pumped the swing one more time, tucked my feet up under me and leaned against the backrest. Grandpa made the swing for me so I would have a place of my own to relax and unwind. That was exactly what I needed to do.

After Jim drove me home from the pond, I only got an hour of sleep. Not nearly enough time to erase the hurt I felt about the joke he played on me.

"Stop thinking about Jim," I said to myself. "Relax and unwind, remember?"

To avoid talking to Grandma and Aunt Maude when I got home, I said good night to George and sneaked upstairs. If they really were in on Jim's joke, I didn't know what to say to them.

I took a deep breath and closed my eyes. The motion of the swing was hypnotic, and I relaxed into its rhythm. If only life were as simple as taking a deep breath and closing my eyes.

"There you are, young lady."

When I heard Grandma's voice I knew it was time to face reality. I opened my eyes, dropped my feet to the ground and looked over at her. She wasn't alone. Aunt Maude was standing beside her.

"Morning," I said.

They walked over to the swing and sat down on either side of me like a pair of bookends. They made sure there was no way for me to escape and avoid them any longer.

"Did you just get home?" Aunt Maude said.

"No."

I looked down at my clothes. I still had on the blouse and shorts I wore to the pond.

"Did you have a good time?" Grandma said.

"No."

"Ye gods, Shirley," she said. "Stop this nonsense and tell us what happened."

I sat up a little straighter and folded my hands in my lap. I didn't want to hurt their feelings, but they deserved an honest explanation.

"All of you played a joke on me, and I didn't think it was funny."

"That's it?" Grandma said. "That's the reason you've been avoiding us?"

"Jimmy worked hard on that surprise," Aunt Maude said. "He must feel awful you didn't like it."

What? She was defending him and not me?

"Thanks to Jim, everybody in town is laughing at me," I said. "I don't know if we can ever be friends again."

Grandma eased off the swing and paced back and forth in front of Aunt Maude and me. When she stopped, she stuffed her hands into the pockets on the sides of her robe, stiffened her back and looked at me.

"Not be friends?" she said. "He's done nothing but be a good friend to you."

"A friend wouldn't make a fool of me."

I felt my bottom lip slip into its pout position. It was a childish habit, but I couldn't seem to fight it.

"Stop that pouting this instant," Grandma said.

I tucked my lip back where it belonged and looked down at my hands. I was too embarrassed to look her in the eye.

"Wasn't he a friend when he duplicated your bedroom at the farmhouse?"

"Yes."

"Wasn't he a friend when he relocated this swing for you?"

"Yes, but—"

"Wasn't he a friend when he made certain you experienced that spectacular meteor shower?"

"Yes, Grandma."

"Jimmy's a good boy," Aunt Maude said. "He'd never hurt you on purpose."

"We all helped him to show you how much he likes you," Grandma said. "If you can't understand that, then maybe he's better off without you."

"Grandma?"

When Aunt Maude reached over and laid her hand on mine, tears welled up in my eyes. I had to bite my bottom lip to keep from crying.

"I acted like an idiot, didn't I?"

"That about sums it up," she said.

Thinking about pushing Jim away and never seeing him again was more than I could bear. I slipped off the swing, threw my arms around Grandma and gave her a long hug.

"I'm so sorry," I said. "I don't know what's happening to me."

"Well, dear," she said, "You're discovering emotions run extremely high when you care for someone."

"You owe Jimmy one big apology, Shirley," Aunt Maude said.

I let go of Grandma, gave Aunt Maude a quick hug and ran to the door. Before I went inside, I turned around.

"I need to borrow Grandpa's truck, Grandma."

"You may use it if you drive carefully."

"I will."

I ran inside, took the stairs two steps at a time and hurried into my room. I snatched the writing tablet off the built-in seat and sat down at the desk.

It didn't take long to write a short note to everyone invited to the wedding ceremony. Other than Irene and Clyde and Grandma, Aunt Maude and I, there were only six. I had enough envelopes in the bottom drawer for all of them.

I wrote their names on the envelopes, stuffed a note in each one and stacked them on the desk. Grandma could deliver the one to Miss Spitz, but I wanted to deliver the rest of them myself.

The idea of driving around the county to deliver invitations made me feel even more tired, but I couldn't rest. If I didn't hurry, Jim and his dad would already be gone for the day before I could get to the mill to deliver theirs.

While I ran the shower and waited for hot water, I went to the closet and picked out clean clothes. I wanted to look my best for Jim. The madras shorts, a sleeveless blouse and white sandals seemed like the perfect outfit to deliver invitations and an apology.

Thirty-three

With the six envelopes in my hand, I rushed downstairs. Grandma and Aunt Maude were at the kitchen table, poring over different sections of the Sunday newspaper.

"I don't have time for breakfast," I said, "and I have to talk to Miss Spitz when I get back."

Grandma peeked over the top of the front section of the paper and nodded. Aunt Maude was too engrossed in the advertising section to even notice me.

"I'm going to go deliver the invitations now."

"That's nice, dear."

"Would you mind delivering one to Miss Spitz for me?"

"I'm certain I'll see her sometime today," she said. "Leave it on the counter."

"Thanks, Grandma."

I put the envelope on the kitchen counter and hurried to the front door. Before I opened it, I looked back at her and Aunt Maude.

Grandma's nose was buried in the paper again, and Aunt Maude never once looked up. I couldn't imagine what they found so interesting in the Sunday edition of the Monticello newspaper.

Even as curious as I was, I was in too much of a hurry to stop and ask them. I knew if I timed my deliveries just right, Jim and his father might still be at home or at the mill.

When I opened the door, I nearly ran into Sarah and Cindy. They were coming from the direction of the bank, and Cindy's hands were full of mail.

"Sarah," I said. "You're just the person I wanted to see."

"I am?"

I shuffled through the envelopes. When I found hers I handed it to her.

"What's this?"

"An invitation for you and Cindy to attend Clyde and Irene's wedding."

"Oh, Mama," Cindy said. "Can we go?"

Sarah turned the envelope over and over in her hands. When she finished examining it, she looked at me and smiled.

"We'd love to come, Shirley."

Cindy jumped up and down and clapped her hands. Her braids flew in all directions with every jump.

"Thanks, Mama."

"There is one favor I need to ask," I said. "Can you do something with Irene's hair before the ceremony?"

Sarah examined the envelope one more time and tucked it inside her dress pocket. She looked at me and smiled even wider.

"Of course," she said. "Consider it our wedding gift to the bride and groom."

I filled her in on the date and time of the wedding and when I needed her at the store. When we finished talking, Cindy wrapped her arms around my waist and gave me a quick hug.

"What was that for?" I said.

"You made my Mama smile."

I was so surprised by her comment I didn't know what to say to her. Instead of saying something stupid, I climbed into Grandpa's truck and waved goodbye to them.

"The rehearsal is at noon on Friday," I said. "We'll go on a picnic afterward."

There were still four envelopes to deliver before I could talk to Jim. I decided the next stop should be to see Pastor Lawrence.

I drove over to the First Community Church, parked at the front curb and walked up to the carved wooden door. Although it was still an hour before services, organ music was playing inside.

When I reached for the handle, the door opened, and Pastor Lawrence stood just inside. He was wearing his usual dress pants and shirt, but he added a suitcoat and tie to the mix.

"Good morning, Shirley," he said. "Come on in."

I went inside and followed him through the narthex to a small office at the side of the church. The music was too loud for us to speak, so he closed the door and motioned for me to sit down.

"I'm sorry to bother you on Sunday, Pastor."

"I have a couple of minutes to spare," he said. "What can I do for you?"

"Clyde and Irene are getting married next Saturday, and I wonder if you'd be available to marry them."

He laughed a little and sat down on his swivel desk chair. He picked up a ballpoint pen from the desk and scribbled on a piece of paper as he spoke.

"I assume this wasn't their idea.

"It was mine," I said. "I didn't want them to go to Monticello and get married by the justice of the peace."

"I've never seen Clyde in church," he said. "How did you get him to agree to a church wedding?"

"I didn't."

"I don't understand."

"Irene wants you to marry them, but she wants the ceremony at the General Store, not the church."

The pastor stopped scribbling and put the pen down. He shook his head and laughed again.

"That sounds just like Irene," he said. "I'd be happy to do the honors no matter where they get married."

I handed him the envelope with his name on it and waited until he read the handwritten note. When he finished, he laid it on the desk.

"I know the invitation is a little informal," I said, "but Irene doesn't want a fancy wedding."

"That sounds like her, too," he said. "Consider the ceremony my gift to both of them."

"Thank you, Pastor," I said. "The rehearsal is at noon on Friday, and there'll be a picnic afterward."

"A picnic?" he said. "Do you have a location in mind?"

"I thought we'd drive over to Lake Sullivan."

"That sounds nice," he said, "but I have another idea."

He grinned at me, leaned back and rocked his chair back and forth. I was almost afraid to ask.

"What's your idea?"

"I haven't shown anyone the place I talked about last summer," he said. "Mind if we go there instead?"

I wasn't comfortable with changing my plans, but if he knew of a better place, why not? It would be fun to see someplace new.

"Okay, Pastor," I said. "Surprise us."

When we stood up, he offered me his hand, and I gave it a quick shake. The proverbial clock was ticking, and we didn't have any more time to visit.

"See you on Friday, Shirley."

I left him in his office and walked back through the narthex to the front door. As I walked outside, the organist was playing a lively rendition of "Go Tell It on the Mountain".

Thirty-four

Once I was back in Grandpa's truck, I glanced down at the last three envelopes on the seat. Since I wouldn't see Mr. Martin until Monday, the next logical one to deliver was Miss Carter's.

I drove down Main Street and turned left onto the county road. When the pavement ended at the edge of town, the truck bumped along the gravel road, kicking up dust.

According to Irene, Miss Carter hired carpenters to add a bathroom in each bedroom upstairs in the old farmhouse. She said the bedroom remodels were beautiful, but I still hated the idea of strangers sleeping in my old room.

When I arrived at Grandma's old driveway, I stopped on the county road and looked up at the house. From that vantage point, everything looked the same outside. The house was still surrounded by old hardwood trees, and Grandma's rose garden was in full bloom.

"Alright, Shirley," I said to myself. "Stalling won't make talking to Miss Carter any easier."

I eased Grandpa's truck up the steep, serpentine driveway and parked near the front door. I was used to going in through the back, but it didn't seem appropriate anymore.

Miss Carter answered the door after I only knocked twice. She was dressed in a beautiful floral muumuu, and her grey-streaked strawberry blond hair hung over her shoulders.

"Yes, Shirley," she said. "How may I help you?"

"I came to give you this invitation and ask you for a couple of favors."

She took the handwritten envelope and turned it over and over in her hands. She didn't open it or make any comment.

"Clyde and Irene are getting married next Saturday," I said. "They would like you to be at the ceremony."

"They would, would they?"

I don't think she believed me, but it didn't matter. Irene was her employee. Inviting her was the proper thing to do, and I really needed her help.

"Let's sit down, shall we?" she said. "The porch is so lovely this time of day."

I was hoping she'd invite me in to see the remodel, but she didn't. She led me across the porch to a group of white wicker chairs facing the corn fields beyond the front yard.

It was nice sitting on the porch again, and the new chairs were comfortable. I just didn't want to visit with her any longer than necessary.

"I know this is short notice," I said, "but I'm looking for a place for the reception."

"I see."

"The café's patio and the empty lot in back would be perfect."

"How many guests are you expecting?"

"At least everyone in town."

I think I heard her gasp. She laid the unopened envelope on a side table and stared at me.

"What will you serve that many guests?"

"It'll be a potluck," I said. "We'll eat whatever food everyone brings."

"How—interesting."

"You won't have to worry about a thing," I said. "I'll go back on Sunday morning and make sure everything is clean and straightened up."

"You mentioned there was something else on your mind."

I cleared my throat and wiggled a little in my chair. She hadn't committed to the reception. I was almost afraid to ask for anything else.

"I see Grandma's roses are in bloom."

"They are."

"Would it be possible to use a few of them for Irene's bouquet and Clyde's boutonniere?"

She looked over at the rose garden and nodded her head. I couldn't read her mind, but that looked like a good sign.

"Is there anything else you require?"

"There is one more thing," I said.

"Well?"

I took a very deep breath and let it out slowly. The last favor was the biggest, and I was afraid it was more than she would be willing to give.

"They can't afford a real honeymoon," I said. "Is your bed and breakfast going to be open on Saturday?"

"It is."

"Would it be possible for them to stay here on their wedding night?"

"How can they afford that?" she said.

"They can't."

Without a word, she stood up and walked over to the railing. Her back was to me, and I was afraid I had gone one step too far. After a minute or two of her silence, I felt obligated to say something.

"Miss Carter?"

She turned around and looked me straight in the eye. A cold shiver went up my spine.

"I agree to every request," she said. "I will consider them my gift to the happy couple."

I jumped up from the chair. I never expected her to agree to everything, and I didn't want to spoil the moment.

"Thank you," I said. "The rehearsal is at noon on Friday."

Before she could change her mind, I hurried off the porch and climbed into the truck. I had no intention of inviting her to the picnic, so I leaned out the window and waved at her.

"See you at the rehearsal, Miss Carter."

I drove slowly down the gravel driveway, trying not to raise much dust. At the county road, I stopped and looked over at the last two envelopes.

Sunday was Jim's and his father's day to get away from the mill, and it was getting late. My chances of catching them before they left were next to non-existent, but I had to try.

I drove back to Willowdale, through town and out to the mill. When I got there, all the doors were closed. Mr. Spencer's truck was gone, and there wasn't any activity at their house.

"Well," I said to myself. "I tried."

Patience wasn't my strong suit, but I didn't have a choice. Like Mr. Martin's envelope, I had to wait one more day to deliver Mr. Spencer's invitation and my apology to Jim.

I turned the truck around and drove back to the store. Grandma was sitting on the sofa closest to the bookcases, reading a book. Aunt Maude and George were nowhere in sight, but I could hear the sound of the television in her apartment.

"Did you get everything done, dear?" Grandma said.

"Not quite," I said. "There's one more thing I have to do today."

I walked to the kitchen, picked up the receiver on the wall phone and waited for the operator. I didn't like involving Miss Spitz in Clyde and Irene's business, but as the town's gossip, she was exactly the person I needed.

"Good morning, Miss Spitz," I said.

"Good morning, Shirley," she said. "How are Marie and Aunt Maude?"

"They're fine, thank you," I said. "I wonder if you could help me."

"Don't you worry," she said. "I know everyone in the county, and I can find whoever you're looking for."

"Thank you, but it's not about that."

There was a long pause. When she came back on the line, she cleared her throat and lowered her voice to a whisper.

"Is it about Mrs. Van Berkel's chickens?"

"What?"

"A fox broke into the coop last night," she said. "It scared the poor chickens so bad, they won't lay their eggs."

"I'm really sorry about her chickens, but it isn't about that either."

"Oh?"

"Clyde and Irene are having a private wedding next Saturday in the General Store," I said. "You'll be getting an invitation, of course."

"Those two are finally getting married?"

"Yes, but there isn't a lot of time," I said. "Do you think you could organize a potluck reception for them?"

There was another long pause. This time when she came on the line, she didn't bother to whisper.

"I'd be happy to help," she said. "What time is the reception?"

"The wedding's at three o'clock, so the reception is right after that."

"Where should everybody take the food?"

"The reception will be on the patio and in the empty lot at Elaine's."

"I'll make sure everybody knows, Shirley."

I had no doubt about that. Nothing stayed a secret for long in a small town, but Miss Spitz would spread the word even faster.

"One more thing," I said. "The rehearsal is at noon on Friday."

"That'll work out just fine," she said. "I'll leave for work right after."

Thirty-five

Mr. Martin sat down on the café's bench and opened the envelope Shirley handed him. When he finished reading the note inside, he wadded it up and tossed it into the trash barrel beside the door.

"Gittin' married, huh?" he said to himself. "Suppose I gotta wear a suit."

He shook his head, pulled a rumpled handkerchief from his pants pocket and blew his nose. The last time he wore a suit was at his wife's funeral.

"No, siree," he said. "Don't even know where it's at."

When Irene walked out of the café, he didn't say a word about a suit. He didn't want her to worry about him and what he was going to wear.

"Got yer weddin' invitation," he said.

"It's kind of spur-of-the-moment."

"Wouldn't miss it."

Her bib apron was stained with bacon grease and sandwich makings and other things he couldn't identify. Her cheeks were flushed and strings of damp hair were stuck to her temples.

"Waitin' for the pastor?" she said.

"Looks like he's runnin' late."

She walked past him, sat on the opposite end of the bench and pulled her braid over her shoulder. When she started twisting the end of it in her fingers, he knew she was thinking hard about something.

"Mr. Martin?"

"Yep."

"There's somethin' I want to ask you."

"What's that?"

He couldn't remember her ever hesitating to ask him about anything before. From the sounds of it, he figured it was pretty important.

"You've known me my whole life," she said.

"Yeah, me an' yer dad were fishin' buddies."

When he looked over at her, she was watching the traffic drive up and down the street. If she had something to say, he wished she'd hurry up and say it.

"What's on yer mind?"

"I've been thinkin'."

"Yeah?"

"What would you say to givin' me away."

He didn't expect her to say that, and he didn't know how to react. Giving away the bride was serious business.

"Ya want me ta give ya ta Clyde at yer weddin'?"

"It'd mean a lot if you'd stand in for my dad."

He took off his old hat and laid it on his lap. He scratched his head and tried to remember where he put his suit and his good pair of shoes.

"I'd be real honored," he said. "But—"

"But what?"

"I'm not buyin' me a new suit."

She turned toward him and laughed. For the first time, he noticed she had her father's smile.

"You can wear whatever you want," she said. "Rehearsal's Friday at noon, and we're havin' a picnic after that."

He nodded his head, picked up his old hat and ran his hankie around the inside of the hatband. When he finished, he put his hat back on and shoved the hankie inside his pants pocket.

"There's Cindy, Mr. Martin," Irene said. "Where do you suppose she's goin'?"

He looked across the street and watched the little girl half-skip, half-walk up the sidewalk. When she got to the corner of the General Store she stopped.

"She surely is one odd young 'un."

"She's not odd," Irene said. "She's findin' her way."

"Ya mean she's lost?"

"Not lost," she said. "She's just tryin' to figure things out."

He watched Cindy creep up to the front of the store and crouch below the front window. After a second, she stood up a little at a time until her eyes were just above the bottom of the window frame.

"If that's not odd, I'll eat my hat," he said.

Irene jumped up, untied her apron and tossed in on the end of the bench. Without a word to him, she stepped off the curb and walked across the street.

He watched as Irene and the little girl sat down on the bench in front of the General Store and talked. After a few minutes, Cindy nodded her head, got up and ran down the sidewalk.

Irene stood up, waited for traffic to pass and walked across the street. She pushed the filthy apron out of her way and sat back down.

"What'd ya say ta her?"

"I asked her somethin' that should help her find her way a little."

"What's that?"

"I asked her to be my flower girl."

Thirty-six

"Come sit down, Jimmy," Bill said. "We can both use the rest."

His son turned over an empty crate and sat down next to his. The sacks of grain they filled were stacked in bins along the back wall and ready for delivery.

"I don't know what I did wrong, Dad."

He looked at his son, peeled off his gloves and rubbed the knuckles on both of his hands. They were red and achy and swollen to twice their normal size.

"I thought it'd be fun to play a little trick on Shirley."

"What kind of trick?"

"I let her think she was sneaking out of the store without her grandma knowing about it."

"Go on."

"It was supposed to be funny, and everybody in town was in on it."

He stopped rubbing his hands and looked at his son again. The boy looked miserable and on the verge of tears.

"She looked like she was having a good time when she saw the meteors."

"What happened?"

His son stood up, walked over to the mill's delivery door and looked out at the ramp. He was a thoughtful boy, but it sounded as though his joke went a little too far afield.

"We started talking about who knew about it."

"Then, what?"

"She got mad and made me take her back home."

He didn't know what to think. Jimmy always treated everyone with respect, but he had a lot to learn about girls. If only his wife were still alive to give their boy some good advice.

"I thought she had a better sense of humor than that."

He shook his head at Jimmy and remembered how hard it was to be young. There were so many lessons to learn, and so little patience.

"I don't think it has anything to do with her sense of humor."

His son spun around, walked back to the crate and sat down again. He looked down at the floor and rubbed a hand across the top of his head.

"What else can it be?"

"Look, son," he said. "You two are fond of each other, aren't you?"

"I thought so."

"It seems to me you broke the cardinal rule."

When his son looked up at him, he could see the frustration on his face. There was no hiding the fact he was hurting inside.

"There's a cardinal rule, Dad?"

"There is."

"What is it?"

"Once you earned Shirley's affection, you needed to treat it like it was something special."

"I thought I did."

"No, son," he said. "It doesn't look that way to me."

"What did I do?"

"You hurt her feelings, and you don't do that to somebody you care about."

"I didn't mean to."

"I know."

His son jumped up, walked over to one of the timber posts and lifted a push broom off a wooden peg. He swept bits of grain and chaff across the floor, and dust flew everywhere.

"Slow down, son," he said. "I can hardly breathe."

He covered his mouth and nose with his hand and tried to keep the dust out. When that didn't work, he struggled to his feet and went outside for a breath of clean air.

Years of milling grain ruined his lungs, and he coughed as hard as he could to clear the dust out of them. When the sound of the broom scraping against the floor stopped, he walked back inside.

"Jimmy," he said. "I'm going to town."

"Okay, Dad."

He grabbed his hat from a peg, put it on and walked outside again. On his way down the dirt loading ramp, he brushed dust and debris from his shirt and pants.

"That boy's going to have it better than me," he said to himself. "I'll see to that."

When he reached the bottom of the ramp, he climbed into his truck and drove down the driveway to the gravel side road. He stopped and waited for another truck coming from the direction of the main road.

When it got closer, he saw it was Horace Wilson's truck. His son was behind the wheel.

Clyde slowed down, turned onto the driveway and pulled to a stop next to him. The young man's arm was resting on the door frame, and he wore a wide smile.

"Jim home, Mr. Spencer?" he said.

"He's sweeping up."

"Good. I have a job for him."

"You have work for my son?"

"Yes, sir."

He didn't know what kind of work his son could do on the Wilson farm. He didn't know anything about crops or heavy machinery or even livestock.

"What kind of work are you thinking?" he said.

Clyde pulled off his cap and kneaded it in his hands. He smiled even wider.

"I want him to be the best man at my wedding."

"You and Irene are getting married?"

"Yes, sir," he said. "I told Jim about it a few of days ago."

"Well, it's about time you tied the knot," he said. "Congratulations."

"Thanks, Mr. Spencer."

He took off his hat, shook his head and laughed at Clyde. Everybody in the whole town knew they were a perfect match. It just took the two of them a lot longer to figure it out for themselves.

"Go on up and see Jimmy," he said. "My boy could use the company."

"Yes, sir."

After Clyde pulled around him and drove up the driveway, he slipped his hat back on. He put his truck in gear, turned onto the side road and headed toward town.

He needed advice, and if anyone could help him, Gene Daily could. Most everybody banked with him, and he had a reputation for knowing everything going on in the county.

"I should find out pretty quick if my idea's a good one or not."

Thirty-seven

After I handed Mr. Martin his envelope, I drove straight to the mill to find Jim. Mr. Spencer's truck was gone, but Clyde's truck stood at the bottom of the ramp.

I parked Grandpa's truck next to it, grabbed the last envelope off the seat and got out. I walked up the steep ramp to the open delivery door and heard Jim and Clyde's voices. They were too far away for me to hear the words, so I decided to play dumb.

"Hello," I said. "Is anybody here?"

When they didn't answer me, I went inside. The air was full of dust, and it reminded me of the last time I was there. I coughed so hard I vowed I would never go there again, but it couldn't be helped. I was on a mission.

"Ignore the filthy air," I said to myself. "You don't have to stay long."

I walked halfway across the main floor and paused to listen. Their voices came from the floor above me, and I remembered how to get up there.

At the back of the room, I found the narrow set of stairs that led to the second floor, and I climbed up. When I reached the top step, I was outside the small room with the jumble of belts and pulleys and wooden chutes. The post and beam construction still reeked with the pungent odor of aged wood, and I almost gagged.

Jim and Clyde were sitting across the room on a belt below one of the chutes. Their backs were turned toward the open doorway, and they couldn't see me standing there. I wasn't sure how to catch their attention, but I wasn't going to wait until they stopped talking.

Without a door to knock on, I rapped my knuckles on the nearest post. That didn't make enough noise for even me to hear. The only option was to use the words.

"Knock, knock."

The two of them jumped down from the conveyor belt and spun around at the same time. When they saw me, their jaws dropped.

"Shirley?" Jim said. "What're you doing here?"

Without a word, I walked over to them and held the envelope out to Jim. When he took it, he studied the names written on the front and laid it on the conveyor belt.

"What is that?"

"It's the official invitation to Clyde and Irene's wedding," I said.

Clyde smiled, looked down and scuffed his shoe against the wooden floor. I suppose I made him uncomfortable, but I had to deliver the envelope while I still had the nerve.

"Hi, Clyde," I said. "How're you doing?"

He raised his head and looked back and forth between Jim and me. His smile grew even wider.

"Jim's going to be my best man."

"That's wonderful," I said. "I can't think of anyone more perfect for the job."

"That's what Irene said."

"Stop it, you two," Jim said. "You're embarrassing me."

"Get over it," Clyde said. "I got to get going."

He wound his way around the equipment and stopped when he reached the top of the stairs. He turned around, put his hand in his shirt pocket and pulled out a scrap of newspaper.

"I'm using this coupon to buy breakfast and celebrate."

"What're you talking about?" Jim said.

"There's an article about Miss Carter in yesterday's paper," he said, "and a big ad in the back."

"What's that have to do with coupons?"

"They're in her ad," Clyde said. "If you take one to the café, you get breakfast half off."

He stuffed the scrap of paper inside his pocket and turned back around. As he started down the steps, he waved.

"Thanks, Jim."

Once Clyde left, the room grew really quiet. Jim didn't say anything, and I didn't know how to begin my apology. To fill the awkward gap, I walked over to the row of windows on the back wall.

The view was as beautiful as I remembered. In the distance, Willow Creek still meandered among the checkerboard of corn and wheat fields. The leaves on some of the willow trees along its bank were already yellow for the fall. Only a few yards away, a diverted stream from the creek still wound its way to the mill's wooden wheel.

"Shirley," Jim said. "Why are you really here?"

I turned around. He looked confused, and I couldn't blame him. The last time he saw me I was mad at him.

"I came to apologize for the other night," I said. "You tried to do something special for me, and I acted like a total idiot."

"Well—maybe not a total idiot," he said.

"Thanks. I think."

He took a few steps closer and smiled at me with his wide, toothy smile. He pulled his cap off his head and slapped it against his pant leg.

"I didn't handle the whole thing very well myself," he said. "I'm sorry I hurt your feelings."

I ran across the floor, wrapped my arms around his neck and gave him a huge hug. He put his arms around me and held on just as tight.

When we finally let go of each other, I couldn't stop smiling. I really had been an idiot and nearly ruined everything.

"Does this mean we're friends again?" he said.

"What do you think?"

Downstairs, a door slammed. After a second or two I heard footsteps and Mr. Spencer's voice.

"You here, son?" he said. "Mr. Ivey's old truck is parked outside."

"Yeah, Dad."

Jim fit his cap back on his head and walked over to the doorway. He stood on the top step and looked down at the first floor.

"Shirley and I are up here."

"You two speaking again?"

"Looks like it," he said. "She brought us a wedding invitation."

I snatched the envelope off the conveyor belt and walked over to Jim. I stood beside him, slipped my hand in his and held the invitation up for his father to see.

"Hi, Mr. Spencer," I said. "I guess friends can't stay mad at each other for very long."

Thirty-eight

Elaine sat down at the front table and spread out her notes. Establishing and maintaining two businesses at once was tedious and time consuming. There never seemed to be an end to the planning.

"Let me see, now," she said. "The rehearsal is on Friday, my bed and breakfast opens Saturday morning, and Clyde and Irene get married Saturday afternoon."

Each event consumed an enormous amount of time, but her situation was much worse than that. She still needed to fill the manager and handyman positions at the bed and breakfast.

She had interviewed several local homemakers and self-employed repairmen. None of them met her strict qualifications. They were neither sophisticated enough nor educated enough to mingle with the type of guests she hoped to attract.

She picked up her pencil to make notes for future interviews, but a knock on the front door distracted her. She tried to ignore the interruption, but the knock came again.

"The café is closed," she said.

Whoever it was had the nerve to knock on the door again. She dropped her pencil, scooted the chair away from the table and stood up.

When she looked out the front window, she saw a young woman about Irene's age standing by the door. Her hair was neatly styled, but her clothes were out-of-date.

"Who in the world can that be?" she said to herself.

Ordinarily, she wouldn't open the door to anyone once the café was closed, but she was curious about the woman. She walked across the room, turned the lock and pulled the door open.

"Hello, Miss Carter."

"Who might you be?"

"I'm Sarah Thomas," she said. "I work at Kut and Kurl."

"I see."

"I heard you're looking for a manager and a cook for your bed and breakfast."

She looked the woman up and down. She was certainly attractive and appeared to be extremely poised. Both pleasant surprises in an unsophisticated town like Willowdale.

"Please, come in and sit down," she said. "We'll begin your interview immediately."

When Sarah sat on the chair facing the window, she sat across from her and pushed aside the paperwork on the table. She tore a sheet of paper from her notepad and wrote Sarah's name at the top.

"Where would you like to begin, Sarah?"

"I make a pretty good breakfast," she said. "I learned from an excellent cook."

"How proficient are you at handling money and communicating with the public?"

"The truth is I have very little experience with either one."

"Oh, dear."

"I finished high school in the top of my class, and I'm a member of the National Honor Society."

"That's admirable, but not very practical."

"All I'm asking is a chance to prove I'm up to the challenge."

She was desperate to fill the position, and Sarah was probably the best candidate she would find in the small town. The woman looked presentable and was intelligent enough to learn the necessary management skills.

"It's been rumored the little girl I see wandering around town is the daughter of a local hairdresser."

"She's my daughter," she said. "Her name is Cindy."

"If you become the manager, you and your daughter will be living on the premises."

"Yes, Miss Carter."

"You will be held personally responsible for any and all of her actions."

"Her actions?"

"I expect your daughter to mind her manners at all times and respect my property and the privacy of my guests."

"Of course, Miss Carter," she said. "I'll make certain she understands the rules."

"Good," she said. "However, I will require a cooking demonstration before you are officially hired."

"Of course."

She glanced at the clock above the magazine rack. It was well past closing, but there was no time to waste. The manager position needed to be filled at once.

"I have time for your cooking demonstration right now, Sarah."

"Yes, Miss Carter."

She tore a blank sheet of paper from the notepad and wrote across it. She stood up, hurried to the counter and found the tape dispenser on a shelf underneath. After she ripped off a piece of the tape, she rushed to the window and stuck the paper to the glass.

"I've reminded everyone the café is closed," she said. "There shouldn't be any interruptions while you prove your cooking skills."

"What would you like me to cook?"

She paused to consider the choices. She had several breakfast favorites, but there were two by which she judged most cooks.

"I believe I would like French toast and scrambled eggs."

"Yes, Miss Carter."

Sarah smiled, got up from the table and went straight to the kitchen. Without hesitation, she tied a clean bib apron over her dress and went right to work.

"Well, Sarah," she said under her breath. "Let's see how your cooking compares to Irene's."

Thirty-nine

While his son walked Shirley to her truck, Bill hung his hat on a wooden peg and turned two crates on their ends. He sat down on one and waited.

After a minute or two, Jimmy came back inside. He was wearing a huge smile.

"So, you and Shirley are speaking to each other again."

"Yeah, Dad."

It wouldn't do any good to press him for more information. He knew his son wouldn't say any more about their relationship until he was good and ready.

"I have some news, Jimmy," he said. "Come sit down."

After his son sat down on the other up-turned crate, he cleared his throat and rubbed his hands together. He was about to turn their world upside down, and he wanted to find the right words.

"This arthritis is getting too bad for me to work here anymore."

"What're you talking about, Dad?"

"I just talked to Gene Daily at the bank, and he's going to help me sell this place."

His son pulled off his cap and ran his hand across the top of his head. His mouth hung open.

"The house, too?"

"No," he said. "I'll live in the house a little while longer."

He could see Jimmy was confused. It was a lot to digest in one bite.

"You'll be too busy with your internship and going to school to even notice," he said.

His son stopped running his hand across his hair and put his cap back on. He got up from the crate and looked down at him.

"I'm sorry, Dad," he said. "I know you and Mom loved this place."

"Don't you be sorry," he said. "Your mother's been gone awhile, and I'm ready for a change."

He eased up from the crate, walked over to his son and put a hand on his shoulder. There wasn't much he could do to help him adjust to the idea.

"What about the house you want me to build out at Mr. Wilson's farm?"

"Oh, I still want you to build that for me someday," he said.

"How long do you suppose it'll take to sell this place?"

He lifted his hand off his shoulder and walked over to the delivery door. He looked out over the ramp and toward his house half-hidden from view by an old willow tree.

"Gene knows somebody who wants to buy it right now," he said. "The guy wants to turn it into an historical site."

"I don't know, Dad," he said. "That makes me feel really old."

He laughed, walked across the room and picked his hat off the peg. When he turned around, his son was sitting on the crate again.

"I have to go out," he said. "I won't be gone long."

"Where are you going?"

"Harriet told me Elaine Carter is looking for a handyman for her bed and breakfast," he said. "I think I'm just the man for the job."

"You sure you want to work for Miss Carter?"

He couldn't blame Jimmy for worrying. In the short time he worked for her, Miss Carter and her niece had been nothing but mean-spirited. His hurt ran deep, and he didn't trust either of them.

"I'm not going to sit around the house and do nothing," he said. "It'll be alright."

"But—"

"Look," he said. "Miss Carter's usually at the café all day, and I probably won't see much of her."

"I hope you're right, Dad."

"If I hurry," he said, "I can catch her before she leaves to go home."

He put on his hat and walked out to his truck. He knew dealing with Elaine Carter would be tricky, but he learned a lot from his son's experience. He'd just do his job, mind his own business and stay out of her way.

Forty

The wedding would be so small the rehearsal didn't take very long. It took longer to rearrange the furniture and tape a sign in the window announcing the library would be closed on Saturday.

"Does anyone have any questions or comments?" the pastor said.

I glanced around the room and saw Irene and Clyde standing between two bookcases, whispering to each other. They were too distracted to ask questions, so I took it upon myself to speak up.

"Remember," I said. "The bride and groom want the ceremony to be casual."

"Shouldn't the flower girl wear something special?" Sarah said.

I looked across the room at Cindy. She was sitting on the floor next to the potbellied stove and reading a comic book to George.

"She'd look perfect in her floral sundress," I said.

"Just how casual is casual?" Mr. Spencer said.

"Wear whatever's comfortable," I said. "Nobody will be dressed up at the reception afterward."

Miss Spitz came to the front of the room and stood next to me. She was holding two of Aunt Maude's chocolate chip cookies in one hand and a cup of coffee in the other.

"I have to get to work," she said. "Tell your grandma I'll get her cup back to her tomorrow."

She left the store before I had a chance to say anything, but I wasn't alone for long. Miss Carter walked up and scowled at me.

"A casual wedding?" she said. "I have never heard of such a thing."

"It's what Irene wants, and that's what she'll get."

I wasn't about to let her sour attitude ruin the happy mood in the room. It was a relief when she turned around and headed for the door. Before she left, however, she looked over her shoulder at me.

"The patio and the empty lot will be ready for the reception tomorrow," she said. "I expect them to be spotless when the café opens on Monday."

"They will be, Miss Carter."

My train was leaving at noon on Sunday. That wouldn't give me much time to do the cleanup before I left, but I didn't mind. It would be worth all the work so Clyde and Irene could have a reception with all their friends.

After she left, I went to the kitchen for hot chocolate to wash the bad taste of our conversation from my mouth. Sally, the first-chair flute player in the high school band, was already there.

"Do you think I sounded okay?"

"I think you were really good," I said. "Clyde and Irene are lucky you can play for their wedding."

"Thanks."

She held her flute case by its handle with one hand and grabbed a handful of cookies with the other. Without saying goodbye to anyone, she turned around and rushed out the door.

Everyone else at the rehearsal stood in front of the book-cases, staring at me. I felt like a specimen on a slide in my biology class at school.

"What?" I said to them. "I just want some hot chocolate."

"No time for that," Jim said. "I'm starving."

"Let's git goin'," Mr. Martin said. "None of us is gittin' any younger."

One by one, we said goodbye to George, patted his head and walked outside. After I gave the little pug one last look, I locked the door and hid the key under the doormat.

It only took a few minutes for us to load the picnic sup-plies and find a ride for everyone. Since Pastor Lawrence wanted us to eat our picnic at a special place he found, he led our little caravan out of town.

Sarah and Cindy rode with me in Grandpa's truck, and I followed right behind the pastor. The farther we drove, the scenery changed from hills covered in corn and wheat fields to rugged terrain with dense woods. Every road we took was gravel, and the old truck kicked up a cloud of dust around us.

"Where're we going, Shirley?" Sarah said.

"I don't know."

"Don't worry, Mama," Cindy said. "This is fun."

It was fun, but the longer we drove, the louder my stomach growled. I began to think a rehearsal picnic wasn't the best idea I ever had.

After an hour's drive, the pastor turned onto a narrow dirt road lined on both sides with thick woods. He slowed down and pulled his car to a stop on a small turnout on the left side of the road.

I stopped Grandpa's truck right behind him, and the other two trucks stopped behind me. The turnout was so narrow, there was barely enough room between Grandpa's truck and the trees to open the driver's door.

When I finally squeezed out of the cab, Pastor Lawrence walked over to me. We stood beside the truck and studied the lay of the land.

"This is it," he said.

The trees on both sides of the road grew close together, and beyond them, the ground rose at a sharp angle. I couldn't see a path anywhere.

"Are you sure this is the right place, Pastor?"

"I'm sure," he said. "We'll park here and go the rest of the way on foot."

Grandma and Aunt Maude walked up to us and stood in front of the pastor. They didn't look happy, and I couldn't blame them.

"Ye gods and little fishes," Grandma said. "How difficult a walk will this be, Albert?"

"It shouldn't be too bad," he said. "What I want to show you isn't very far from here."

When the rest of the group walked up, Mr. Martin grumbled, pulled a hankie from his pants pocket and blew his nose. The rest of them looked excited about the adventure, but I reserved my opinion for later.

"Let's get things unloaded," Mr. Spencer said. "I think we can all use some food."

"Good idea," Jim said.

There was a small patch of grass among the trees only a few feet from the road. Jim and I carried the church's folding chairs over to it and set them up. Everyone else carried blankets and picnic baskets and Mr. Spencer's cooler.

"Did you make the sandwiches, Grandma?"

"Not today," she said. "For a special occasion such as this, Maude prepared our lunch."

"Thank yer lucky stars," Mr. Martin said.

"Yeah, Aunt Maude," Irene said. "Thanks."

Without a word, the pastor turned toward her and Clyde and nodded his head. Then, he looked at the rest of us and nodded his head again.

"I see everyone wore sturdy shoes," he said.

We all looked around at each other's feet. My saddle oxfords were definitely sturdy, but I couldn't imagine why I would need them.

"What's so important about our shoes?" Jim said.

"Yes, Albert," Grandma said. "Why are you suddenly concerned about our footwear?"

"You'll see when we get there," he said. "That's all I'm going to say."

I wanted to know more about his plan, but I didn't ask any questions. Instead, I ate my ham and cheese sandwich, drank my pop and wondered what he was up to. Whatever it was, it sounded as though we were in for an endurance hike, not a stroll.

Forty-one

After we finished eating, Pastor Lawrence grabbed a gym bag from the trunk of his car and started up the dirt road. All of us followed behind him in groups of two or three.

The only exception was Cindy. She ran a few yards ahead of him and stopped until he caught up to her.

"What's the bag for?" she said.

"It's part of the surprise."

"Can I see what's in it?"

"Then it wouldn't be much of a surprise, would it?"

Cindy didn't say anything else. She ran ahead of him again and waited a few yards away.

"Don't you get too far ahead of us," Sarah said.

Only half a mile into our hike, we were stopped by a massive mudslide blocking the road. A wide swath of bare earth marked where it slid down the steep hillside, shoving boulders and up-rooting trees in its path. After baking in the sun all summer, the dirt was as solid as concrete around all the debris.

"Ye gods, Albert," Grandma said. "This is certainly a more rugged walk than you led me to believe."

"I guess we should turn around and go back," Aunt Maude said.

The pastor looked up and down the other side of the road and the hillside beyond it. When he turned around, he looked at each of us and smiled.

"That won't be necessary," he said. "Follow me."

He turned back around, walked off the edge of the road and disappeared among the trees with the bag in his hand. I only hesitated for a second before following him.

"Wait up," I said. "I'm coming."

The pastor walked so fast, I lost sight of him as soon as I stepped into the woods. There wasn't a real path through the underbrush, but he left behind a winding trail of trampled grass and weeds.

I was only a few yards up the makeshift path when I heard Jim's voice. I stopped and waited for him to catch up to me.

"Hey, Shirley."

"I'm over here."

While I waited, I checked my watch. It was only three o'clock, but it looked more like dusk under the heavy tree canopy. Even the air felt cooler than it did out on the road.

In less than a minute, Jim ran up and stood beside me. He was so out of breath, he bent over, rested his hands on his knees and panted.

"Are you alright?" I said.

"I'm—great," he said. "What's—your—hurry?"

"I want to see what's in that gym bag."

I only waited a minute for him to catch his breath. Then, he followed me along the path the pastor left.

"How many of the others are coming?" I said over my shoulder.

"Everybody except my dad, your grandma, Aunt Maude and Mr. Martin," he said. "They went back to guard the picnic stuff."

"They think it'll get stolen out here in the middle of nowhere?"

"I think it has to do with bears."

"Bears?"

"Yeah," he said. "They're foraging for anything they can find before they hibernate."

I stopped and hugged my arms to my chest. I turned in a slow circle, studying the space between the trees, and my imagination went wild. Every stump and every clump of grass looked like a bear.

"Grandma told me they aren't usually aggressive."

"They aren't," he said, "unless you get between them and their cubs or food."

That didn't make me feel any safer. I had seen bears in the zoo, and they were big and powerful. Just the thought of them wandering in the woods with us was enough to send chills up my spine.

"Are we going to be alright out here?"

"I think so," he said.

While I thought about his answer, the rest of the group wound their way toward us. Clyde and Irene were in the lead, smiling at each other and holding hands. Cindy and her mother were right behind them, picking colorful leaves off the ground.

None of them seemed concerned about the wildlife, but I couldn't help myself. By the time they caught up to us, I was in a near panic. I wanted to run back to the picnic area and hide in Grandpa's truck.

"Is everybody okay?" I said.

Clyde looked straight at my eyes. I wasn't good at hiding my feelings, and I probably looked scared.

"Why wouldn't we be okay?" he said.

"Just ignore her," Jim said. "She's not used to the woods."

Cindy pushed her way around Sarah, stood beside me and smiled. Her arms were scratched from wild rose thorns, but she didn't appear to have a care in the world.

"Don't worry, Shirley," she said. "We won't let anything happen to you."

It was nice of her to try and comfort me, but I wasn't looking for sympathy. I only wanted us to see the pastor's surprise without getting eaten alive.

"Let's just go, okay?" I said.

Jim adjusted his baseball cap, stepped around me and stood in front of all of us. We lined up single file behind him and followed the meandering path the pastor left.

When we reached the foot of a steep rise, we found the pastor waiting for us. He was standing near a pile of dead brush, and the gym bag was on the ground beside him.

"There you are," he said. "I was beginning to think no one wanted to see my surprise."

"Not a chance," Clyde said.

Cindy walked over to the pastor and looked up at him. Her hands were full of leaves.

"Where's the surprise?"

"Behind the brush," he said, "but we need to move it first."

I was confused. Did he expect us to clean up the woods, or was this a lesson in teamwork?

"Clyde and Jim," he said. "You two drag that brush pile out of the way."

"Yes, sir," Jim said.

While they moved the brush, the pastor bent down and un-zipped the bag. Cindy knelt down beside it, dropped her leaves on the ground and looked inside.

"There's nothing but flashlights in here."

"That's right, Cindy," he said. "Lots of them."

I was starting to worry about the pastor's sanity. Why would he carry around a bag full of flashlights? It was darker under the trees than on the road but not dark enough for that.

"How come we need flashlights?" Irene said.

"Because it's going to get dark very soon."

I looked up at the tops of the trees. There were small patches of sky visible through the thick canopy, and every patch was blue.

"It's still early," I said. "We shouldn't have to worry about it getting dark."

"Oh, but you will," he said. "Everybody will need two flashlights."

"Even me?" Cindy said.

"Everybody," he said.

Once Jim and Clyde had the brush moved away, Pastor Lawrence picked up the bag. We walked over to the boys, and I saw a gaping hole at the base of the hill.

"What is this, Pastor?" I said.

"I discovered this opening on one of my hikes last summer," he said. "I hid it with brush so nobody else would find it."

"An opening for what?" Sarah said.

"You'll see."

Jim and I walked over to the hole and tried to look inside. It was too dark to see beyond the first foot or two.

"You mean you want us to go in there?" Jim said.

"I do, and I think you'll be pleasantly surprised."

Irene leaned against Clyde's arm, pulled her braid over her shoulder and twisted the end. Her eyes were as wide as I had ever seen them.

"I'm supposed to squeeze through that little hole?" she said.

"It'll be okay," Clyde said. "I'll help you."

Jim and I stepped away from the hole to give the pastor some room. He picked up two of the flashlights, tucked one under his belt and held the other in his hand.

"Just do what I do," he said. "I'll be waiting for you on the other side of the opening."

"Is it safe for Cindy?" Sarah said.

"It should be," he said. "Just keep her close to you."

"Did you hear that, Cindy?"

"Yes, Mama."

After Pastor Lawrence disappeared into the hole, Sarah and her daughter took turns crawling inside. That left four of us, and we looked back and forth at each other.

"Clyde," Jim said. "You and Irene go next."

Clyde went first, and Irene went in right after him. I didn't hear any complaints from her, so I assumed she made it through alright.

I picked up two flashlights and stuffed one in the back waistband of my jeans. I eased onto my hands and knees and switched on the other flashlight.

"Here goes, Jim," I said. "If I don't get back, tell Grandma I love her."

"Tell her yourself," he said. "I'll be right behind you if you need help."

I took a deep breath and crawled into the dark hole. As I inched my way across the damp dirt, I swung the flashlight back and forth. The beam was only strong enough to reach three or four feet ahead of me.

The farther I went, the dirt and the air turned cooler, and the space around me grew tighter and tighter. Soon, there was only enough room to lie on my stomach and elbow walk my way forward.

"I don't think I can do this," I said.

Someone ahead of me flashed a light in my face, and I squinted at it. As harsh as the light was, it was comforting to know someone was there for me.

"You're almost here, Shirley," Clyde said.

Keeping my head low, I concentrated on his beam of light. I crawled ahead a few more feet until I saw his hand reaching for me.

I grabbed it and held on with all my strength. I ducked my head to keep a low profile, and he pulled me the rest of the way through.

"Yuck," I said and spit dirt from my mouth.

"You okay?"

"Yeah, I'm fine," I said. "Thanks for the help."

I struggled to my feet and brushed dirt off my blouse and jeans. I wondered if I could have even gotten through without Clyde.

"Welcome to my cave, Shirley," the pastor said.

All around me was total darkness except for small dots of light from the other flashlights. Even though I knew I was surrounded by friends, I felt isolated, and I swung my light around to see them.

Clyde was prone on the ground in front of the hole, and Irene stood next to his feet. Sarah was a few feet away, holding Cindy's hand. Pastor Lawrence stood next to them.

When I was satisfied I wasn't really alone, I directed my light at my feet. I was on solid ground, and I took a step in Sarah's direction. Before I could take a second step, the pastor shined his light on my face.

"Don't move, Shirley," he said.

"Why?"

"You'll see as soon as Jim gets here."

I stood very still and turned my light on the passage hole, looking for him. After a minute or two, he crawled out of the hole without Clyde's help and stood up.

I was tempted to run over there and stand with him, but I didn't. I forced myself to stay where I was and be a good example for Cindy.

"Now that we're all here," the pastor said, "stay right where you are, and I'll shine my light around for you."

He pointed his flashlight's beam straight above his head, and I looked up. Stalactites of every size hung from the ceiling like icicles.

"As far as I'm aware," he said, "I'm the first person to know about this cave."

"Wow," Cindy said. "I didn't know we had caves."

"There's all kinds of them around here," Clyde said.

When the pastor pointed his flashlight at his feet, I understood why he didn't want us to move. We were on a narrow ledge barely large enough to hold the seven of us. Beyond the ledge was complete darkness.

Forty-two

"Slowly turn in place," the pastor said. "You'll get a pretty good idea of what's around you."

We did what he said and shined our lights all around. With so many beams pointed in so many directions, I saw how enormous the cave was.

"Do you hear that?" I said.

Somewhere there were plinking noises. They sounded like leaky faucets dripping into a tub of water. I couldn't tell which direction the noises came from, but they sounded close by.

"It seems I discovered a living cave," the pastor said.

I pointed my light at my feet and followed the outline of the ledge. A few feet to the right of me, a series of smaller ledges led downward like stair steps.

"Maybe those go to the cave floor, Pastor."

"One day," he said, "I'll come back with proper equipment and do some exploring."

While everyone else shined their lights across the ceiling, I kept my beam on the small ledges. One small step at a time, I moved closer to them to get a better look.

Their surfaces looked smooth and shiny in the flashlight's beam, and their front edges had a slight downward tilt. All around them was nothing but black space.

"I've seen enough, Pastor," Sarah said. "I need to get Cindy out of here."

"I understand you're concerned for your daughter," he said, "but if you leave, we all have to leave."

There was a lot of grumbling from everybody when he said that, but I was too busy to listen to them. My curiosity drew me farther away from the group until I was looking straight down on the small ledges.

I shined my light from the top one down to the bottom one. Just as I suspected, they led to the cave floor, and the plinking sounds were louder from where I stood.

"Okay, okay," Sarah said. "I don't want to spoil all the fun."

"Thanks, Mama."

I turned around to tell them about the ledges, but I didn't get the chance. My right shoe slipped on the smooth limestone and spun me around.

Both of my feet flew out from under me, and I lost my grip on the flashlight. It went flying over the edge into the dark abyss. I landed on my back on the first small ledge.

"Oh, no—"

"Shirley!"

I hit so hard the metal flashlight at my back broke free. It bounced all the way down the ledges and hit the floor with a loud thump.

Without a flashlight, I couldn't see anything around me. I felt along the stone in the pitch black and guessed how close I was to the edge.

When I felt confident enough, I rolled onto my stomach. I waved my hand in front of me, trying to find the lip of the large ledge. It was no use. It was out of my reach.

I clawed at the limestone, trying to pull myself up. The stone was just too smooth for me to get a grip. The more I struggled, the farther down I slipped.

To try to stop my momentum, I pushed my hands and the toes of my shoes against the stone. It didn't help. I slid faster and faster.

I slipped off the first small ledge and belly-flopped onto the next. Like a sled, I gained speed and slipped from one ledge to another. Each time my stomach hit, the jolt nearly knocked all the wind out of me.

"Shirley," Jim said. "Talk to me!"

As I fell, his voice sounded farther and farther away as if I were in a dream. I tried to answer him, but I couldn't draw a full breath.

I lost count of how many ledges I bounced off. I only knew the toes of my shoes finally touched the cave floor. I skidded to a stop next to a gigantic stalagmite.

"Shirley," Jim said. "Are you alright?"

He shined his flashlight on me from the top ledge, and I looked to one side. My extra flashlight was only inches away from me. I stretched my arm out, grabbed it and turned it on.

The other flashlight landed several feet across the floor. As I watched it, the beam turned dim, flickered twice and went out.

"Shirley, say something."

I pushed myself onto my hands and knees, turned over and sat on the floor. I used my light to check for injuries, but there didn't seem to be anything major.

There were a few cuts and scrapes on my legs and arms, and the knees on my jeans were ripped. There were blood stains all around the jagged holes in the denim.

"I don't think I broke anything."

"Thank goodness for that," he said, "but what were you thinking?"

The cave floor was cold and damp, and I was already getting stiff from the fall. Discussing my stupidity was the last thing I wanted to do.

"All of you stay away from the edge," I said. "One of us down here is enough."

I swung the beam of my flashlight around the floor of the cave. More stalagmites rose from the floor around me.

A pool of water was only a few feet away, and I shined my light across its surface. I couldn't tell how deep it was, but small droplets rolled off the stalactites above it. Each time they hit the water, they made a plinking sound.

"At least I found the source of the noise, Pastor."

"That's not funny," he said. "We need to figure a way to get you out of there."

"Are you really okay, Shirley?" Cindy said.

"I'm fine."

I stood up and shined my light on the base of the jagged wall in front of me. I moved the light upward until I found the large ledge where everyone stood. They were looking down at me, but they were too far above me to reach over the edge and pull me up.

"Don't worry," Clyde said. "Me and Jim will go for help."

"Wait," I said. "Mrs. Van Berkel's old rope is in Grandpa's truck."

"Anything else?" Jim said.

I shivered and folded my arms across my chest. My skin was clammy and covered with goose bumps.

"I could use my sweater."

"You got it," he said. "We'll be back as fast as we can."

Clyde gave Irene a big hug before he went out of sight. Jim knelt down and looked over the edge at me.

"Stay right where you are," he said, "and no funny business."

"Where would I go?" I said. "What do you mean by funny business?"

"I mean stay where you are and don't get close to that water."

"Go on, Jimmy," the pastor said. "I'll keep a close eye on her."

Jim looked at me for another second or two. Then, he stood up and disappeared from sight.

Even though he just left, I missed him. I didn't feel as safe or as brave without him there.

253

"I think I should take Cindy out of here," Sarah said.

"No, Mama, I want to stay and help."

"Just what do you think you can do?"

There was a long pause. I could only imagine how hard Cindy tried to think up a good excuse to stay.

"Shirley's all alone, Mama," she finally said. "She needs somebody to talk to."

"She can talk to the pastor or Irene."

"It's not the same thing."

I shined my light across the ledge. Sarah and Cindy were so far back from the edge, I could barely see the tops of their heads.

"I've never lived on a farm," I said. "I'd like to hear more about that."

"Please, Mama," Cindy said. "I have lots of stories I can tell."

She and her mother walked into the beam of my flashlight and sat down a few feet from the edge. When they pointed their lights at me, I moved my own light a little higher. Pastor Lawrence and Irene were standing right behind them.

"I'm not goin' anywhere," Irene said.

"I'm not either," the pastor said. "I got us into this mess, and I'm staying right here until we all leave."

I felt relieved all of them were staying, and I smiled at them in spite of my wobbly knees. I wanted to sit back down, but the limestone was too cold for that. Instead, I stood next to the water, listened to the rhythmic plinking sounds and did what I learned in Tai Chi class.

I took in one deep, cleansing breath and let it out slowly. With the next breath, I closed my eyes and let my mind wander.

I pictured the five of us on the overstuffed sofas in Grandma's library, sipping cambric tea. George was asleep next to the potbellied stove, and Aunt Maude was in the kitchen baking cookies. I could almost smell the chocolate chips.

"You ready for a story, Shirley?" Cindy said.

"Huh?"

"Are you ready for a story?"

I forced myself to leave my beautiful dream and return to my cold, damp reality. When I opened my eyes, all their flashlights were trained on me.

"I'm ready, Cindy."

"Well," she said, "everybody knows about roosters."

"They wake you up, right?"

"Kind of, but hardly anybody knows how to slop hogs."

She picked exactly the right topic to capture my attention. I had never given slopping hogs a thought before.

"I sure don't know how to do that," I said. "Tell me."

Forty-three

"Ye gods and little fishes, Shirley," Grandma said. "You assured me you would never take risks like that again."

She set a tray of drinks and the last of the picnic sandwiches on the coffee table and sat next to Aunt Maude. I was on the sofa across from them with Irene and Sarah, and I tried to avoid eye contact with her.

"I didn't mean to fall, Grandma," I said. "The ledges were slipperier than I thought."

"Well, young lady, you're very fortunate the doctor gave you a clean bill of health."

"Except for her cuts," Sarah said.

It seemed as though it had taken the boys forever to get back to the cave. When they finally did, Clyde dropped my sweater to me. I put it on and tucked my two flashlights into the waistband of my jeans.

After Jim tied a loop in the end of the old rope, he knelt down and lowered it to me. I slipped my arms through the loop and secured it around my back and under my armpits.

I leaned against the loop and held onto the knot while Jim and Clyde hauled me up a little at a time. I used my feet to push against the jagged wall to keep from scraping against the rough limestone.

Pastor Lawrence and Irene coiled the slack end of the rope and kept it from entangling the boys' legs. Sarah and Cindy pointed their flashlights at us and the edge so no one else would tumble over.

By the time the seven of us crawled through the passage and hiked back to the vehicles, they were already loaded. Everyone found his original ride, and we drove in the caravan back to the General Store.

I showered and changed clothes while everyone else unloaded the supplies and Grandma called Dr. Thompson. He hurried right over, slathered iodine on my cuts and covered them with bandage strips.

If I didn't look ridiculous enough, purple bruises appeared all over me. I looked like a cross between a tattered rag doll and a grape.

"I hope I'll look okay for your wedding tomorrow, Irene."

"It's a miracle you're not hurt bad," she said. "A few bandages are nothin'."

"She's right," Sarah said, "and it's over now. I think we should talk about something else."

Each of us took a plate and picked up a ham and cheese sandwich. While we ate, we talked about Clyde and Irene's wedding, and Grandma finally relaxed. She ate her whole sandwich and never spoke of the accident again.

In the kitchen, all the men were seated at the table playing penny ante poker. Each of them had a dollar's worth of pennies stacked in front of him.

They were so busy with the game it looked to me as though they barely touched their sandwiches. Even the bowl of apples and the bag of potato chips on the counter looked untouched.

"If ya ask me," Mr. Martin said. "It's a day fer the books."

"Stop talking, old man, and deal," Mr. Spencer said.

"Don't ya rush me, ya whippersnapper."

Listening to them made me understand my grandpa a little better. His Friday night games at the café had been more than about poker. They had been about relaxing the rules and sharing time with good friends.

I was sorry Grandma donated his poker table to the Central Indiana Men's Association, but it couldn't be helped. There was no room for it anywhere in the store.

"Well, I'm stuffed," I said.

I set my empty plate on the coffee table and looked over at Cindy beside the potbellied stove. She was sitting next to George, eating an apple and re-reading her comic book.

"I'll be right back."

I stood up, grabbed a cup of hot chocolate from the tray and walked over to the stove. I ignored my sore muscles and eased onto the floor on the other side of George.

"That's quite the woman," I said, pointing to the book.

Cindy looked up at me and smiled. Her striped T-shirt and tattered jeans were smudged with dirt, but thanks to Grandma's rule, her hands were clean.

"She's a hero," she said.

"She's only a comic book character," I said. "Real people don't need super powers or fancy costumes to be heroes."

She laid her half-eaten apple on the floor, closed the book and laid it on her lap. The corners on the cover were dog-eared from her handling it so much.

"I know that," she said. "You're real, and you're a hero."

"Why do you say that?"

"You saved my life at the lake."

I took a long drink of my hot chocolate and thought about what to say. It was clear the time had come to set her straight about a few things.

"I did what needed to be done," I said. "I used what I learned in my lifesaving class to help you and the other people."

"You took a class?"

"Of course, and you can, too, when you're a little older."

"So I can be a hero?"

"We don't help people because we want to be heroes."

"We don't?"

"Absolutely not," I said. "We help people because it makes us feel good to do something special for someone else."

Cindy leaned over and ran her hand down George's side. The comic book slipped off her lap, but she didn't seem to notice.

"How did you get so smart?"

"I take other classes and read a lot of books."

"What kind of books?"

"Well," I said. "I read books about everything."

"Why?"

"I love to learn," I said. "Someday, I might even use all that knowledge to help somebody."

"Does your grandma have books about that stuff?"

"She has lots of them."

Cindy stopped petting George, sat up straight and looked over at the bookcases. Her eyes were open wide, and her face practically glowed.

"You know, Cindy," I said. "Today, you're my hero."

"I am?"

She looked back at me and smiled. I had her full attention again.

"You stayed in the cave with me and told me stories about living on a farm."

"That wasn't special," she said. "I just talked a lot."

She was right about that. I was surprised one little girl could have so many stories.

"Listening to you kept me from being scared while we waited for help."

"Anybody could've told you stories."

"Maybe, but nobody else did, did they?"

She knee-walked over to me and threw her arms around my neck. She squeezed so hard I thought my face would turn blue.

"Hey," I said. "A person has to breathe."

She let go of me and giggled. It was a beautiful sound, but there was one more thing I needed to say.

"There's something you must always remember, Cindy."

"What?"

"Real heroes never brag about the good things they do."

"But how will anybody know what they did?"

"They probably never will."

"Oh."

I drank the last of my hot chocolate, gave George a scratch behind his ears and struggled up off the floor. Cindy had a lot to think about, and I hoped what I said helped to end her hero worship of me.

On my way back to the sofa, I watched the men gather up their pennies. Clyde was the first to stand up. He handed the deck of cards to Mr. Martin and slapped him on the shoulder.

"Keep these," he said. "Don't think I'll be playing poker for a while."

"Ya keep 'em," Mr. Martin said. "I'm countin' on ya fer next Friday."

I had to laugh. Clyde was getting married in one day. I suspected Irene would have something to say about the poker game.

"Shirley," Sarah said. "Come sit down."

I set my cup on the coffee table and plopped down between her and Irene. I kicked off my moccasins, tucked my legs up under me and rested my head on the back cushion. My muscles were so stiff I wasn't sure I would ever get up again.

"Thank you for what you said to Cindy," Sarah said. "You're already a good teacher."

"You heard all of that?"

"We all heard it, dear," Grandma said.

I rolled my head to the right and looked across the room at Cindy. She gave George a pat on his head, picked up the comic book and apple and got up off the floor. She waited for the men to parade past her and out the front door before she took the book back to the library.

"Will you look at that," Aunt Maude said.

I twisted around and looked over the back of the sofa. Cindy wasn't near the young readers' area like I expected. She was wandering down the narrow aisle, eating her apple and looking up and down at all the shelves.

Maybe what I said encouraged her to think about other books besides comics. At least I hoped it did.

"Alright, ladies," Grandma said. "It's time for us to call it a day, too."

She pushed herself up from the sofa, gathered the dirty cups and uneaten sandwiches and stacked everything on the tray. When she started toward the kitchen, Sarah stood up and took the tray from her.

"You've done enough for today," she said. "Shirley and I will clean up the kitchen."

"That's very thoughtful of you both," Grandma said and flopped back down beside Aunt Maude.

The last thing I wanted to do was help clean up, but Sarah didn't give me a choice. By the time she got to the kitchen, I managed to unfold my legs. I stood up and reached for the arm of the sofa to steady myself.

Just as I was about to take my first step, Irene jumped up from the sofa. It didn't take a genius to figure out why. Clyde was standing at the open front door with a silly grin on his face.

"Clyde's waitin' to take me home," she said. "Sorry about the dishes."

"Nonsense," Grandma said with a wave of her hand. "The bride doesn't do dishes the night before her wedding."

"You ready to go?" Clyde said.

"You'd better get going," Aunt Maude said. "You don't want to keep your groom waiting."

Neither Grandma nor Aunt Maude bothered to get up from the sofa and walk her to the door. They pulled off their shoes and put their feet up on the coffee table.

We all deserved to relax after the day we had, but I forced my achy body to the kitchen. I grabbed a dishtowel from the counter and dried the first glass Sarah washed.

The longer I stood, the more I hurt, and I was anxious to get off my feet. The problem was Sarah. She washed the dishes at a snail's pace until I couldn't stand it anymore.

"I'll finish up here," I said. "You and Cindy go home."

"Thanks, Shirley," she said and dropped the dishrag into the soapy water. "We'll be here in plenty of time tomorrow to fix Irene's hair."

"Why don't you and Cindy come for breakfast," I said. "Saturday is Aunt Maude's pancake day."

"Thanks, but we can't," she said. "I start my job at the bed and breakfast tomorrow morning."

"Of course," I said. "I'm really glad you got the job."

"Me, too."

I tossed the dishtowel beside the sink, leaned against the kitchen counter and watched Sarah round up her daughter. She had to practically drag Cindy away from the bookshelves and over to Grandma and Aunt Maude.

"Thank you both for inviting us to spend the day with you," she said.

Cindy elbowed her way in front of her mother and smiled. She stood up so straight she looked as though she had grown two inches since our little talk.

"Thanks for the sandwich and the apple," she said. "They were really good."

"You are most welcome," Grandma said. "We were happy you could join us."

"See you tomorrow," Aunt Maude said, leaned her head against the back of the sofa and closed her eyes.

On their way out the front door, Cindy looked over her shoulder and threw me a wave. I waved back and sighed with envy. I wanted to call it a day, too, but I still had dishes to wash.

Forty-four

I turned back around and stuck my hands in the hot, soapy water. The bottom of the dishpan was lined with glasses, and I pulled out one of them to scrub.

"Hey, Shirley."

"Jim?"

I looked up and saw him at the back of the room standing in the arched doorway. I didn't know why he came in through the back door, but he was clutching a shopping bag in his hand.

"Got a minute?" he said.

When he smiled, I dropped the glass back into the soapy water and glanced over my shoulder at the sitting area. Aunt Maude's eyes were still closed, but Grandma looked at me and nodded her head.

"Just a short visit, young lady," she said. "You need your rest for tomorrow."

"Yes, Grandma."

I pushed myself away from the counter, dried my hands on the dishtowel and made my way over to him. My muscles ached with every step, but I didn't let that stop me.

"Let's go out back," he said. "I brought you your souvenirs."

Before we started for the backyard, George got up from his blanket and padded over to us. He bumped into Jim's leg, looked up at him and wagged so hard his whole body wiggled.

"Can he go, too?" I said.

"Wouldn't go without him."

He handed me the shopping bag, scooped up George and tucked him under his arm. He held his other hand out to me, and we walked hand in hand through the back hallway.

When we got to the back door, Jim let go of my hand, and we went outside. He walked over to the swing and set George on the seat. I followed right behind him, put the shopping bag on the ground and sat next to the little pug.

"Let's see what we have here, Shirley," he said.

He dug into the bag and pulled out two bundles wrapped in Christmas paper. He handed me the one with snowmen all over it.

"Sorry about the wrapping paper," he said. "It's all I had."

"It's perfect, Jim."

"Go ahead and unwrap it."

I tore at the paper, and I was surprised at what was inside. It was a two-feet-long pennant from Purdue.

"Purdue?" I said. "I'm not going to Purdue."

"It'll make more sense to you in a second."

He handed me the other package wrapped in paper covered with Christmas trees. I tore it open and found a two-feet-long pennant from Ball State. At least that one made sense to me, but I still didn't understand.

"Two pennants?" I said.

"My friend, Andy, went to Muncie awhile back," he said. "I asked him to buy a Ball State pennant for me while he was there."

"Okay."

I held up the two pennants by the edges with the ties and looked back and forth at them. They both had school logos and bold lettering in school colors.

"They're really pretty, Jim."

"Don't you get it?" he said.

"Guess not."

"Hang those on the wall behind your desk in the dorm."

"Then, what?"

"You'll see them every time you sit down to study," he said.

"And they'll remind me of you?"

"They'll remind you of us."

I put the pennants on the seat and jumped down from the swing. I threw my arms around his neck and hugged him as hard as I could.

"These are the best souvenirs in the world," I said. "Thank you."

"Just one more thing," he said.

After he unwound my arms from his neck, he held my hands, leaned down and kissed me. It was just as gentle as the first kiss, and my heart raced just as fast as the first time.

When he stopped and stood up straight again, the back door swung open with a bang. He let go of my hands, and we looked over at the door. Grandma was standing there with her hands on her hips, watching us.

"It's time to come in, Shirley," she said.

"We'll be right there, Grandma."

I was embarrassed, but Jim didn't seem bothered. He smiled at me, picked up the pieces of wrapping paper and stuffed them into the shopping bag.

I had hoped Grandma would give us more time to spend together. After all, I was leaving in two days, and we might not have another chance to be alone.

"Right this minute, young lady," she said and slammed the door closed behind her.

"Sorry about that," I said. "She can be old-fashioned about these things."

"That's okay," he said. "I'll see you again tomorrow."

He picked up George and held him under his arm like a football. When he reached his hand out to me, I took it and held on tight.

I picked up the pennants with my other hand, laid them in the bag with the paper and looped my arm through the handle. Not easy to do one-handed, but I wasn't about to let go of Jim.

As we walked together toward the back door, the porch light clicked on. It wasn't quite dark enough outside for that, but I knew what it meant. Grandma wanted us inside immediately.

Forty-five

"I see you are living up to your end of our bargain, Shirley."

Miss Carter stood on the top step in front of the French doors and looked down at me. I gripped the broom handle a little tighter and waited for her inevitable criticism.

"However," she said. "I expect the chairs and tables to be returned to their proper locations."

I knew she wouldn't be satisfied with my work. She was never satisfied with anyone's work, and I forced myself not to overreact.

"Of course," I said. "I'll make sure everything's put back the way you had it."

"I certainly hope so."

"Yes, Miss Carter."

"By the way," she said, "the red roses you requested at the wedding are on the lunch counter."

"Thank you for bringing them."

She straightened her back, lifted her chin and looked over the top of the patio fence. While she scanned the empty lot, I laid the comic section of the Saturday newspaper on the limestone pavers. I swept a pile of dirt and yellow rose petals onto it.

I smiled to myself and thought about what Mr. Martin taught me my first summer in Willowdale. If I had to sweep the debris onto a paper anyway, I might as well have something fun to read.

"You haven't tidied up the empty lot, I see," she said.

"I was leaving that for last."

"When did you say your train is departing?"

I leaned the broom against the edge of the closest table. I bent down, picked up the paper and debris and looked up at her.

"I'll have enough time to finish."

"Make certain you do," she said. "I have an errand to run, but I'll return later to inspect your work."

"Yes, Miss Carter."

She glanced at the patio one last time, turned around and walked into the café. I didn't relax until the French doors closed behind her.

"You don't have anybody to blame for this but yourself, Shirley," I said under my breath.

I looked at my watch. The train was arriving at noon, and that didn't give me much time to finish. Thankfully, the café was closed on Sunday, and I had the place to myself.

I plopped down on the chair next to the broom and set the paper on the table. Miss Carter and I were the only ones who knew about the bargain I struck with her. As much as I disliked our arrangement, I did it for Clyde and Irene.

Their wedding had gone almost exactly as planned. Irene looked radiant in her white lace sundress and white flats. She carried a bouquet of Grandma's yellow roses with a white satin ribbon tied around the stems.

Sarah styled her hair by winding her braid into a huge bun on the top of her head. The finishing touch was a single yellow rose attached to the side of the bun.

Clyde looked all cleaned up for a change. Instead of his usual bib overalls, he wore a pair of khaki pants and a laundered plaid shirt. A yellow rose bud was pinned to the collar, and his hair was slicked back from his face. He even traded his old work boots for a new pair of tennis shoes.

As the best man, Jim wore khaki pants and a short-sleeved dress shirt without a tie. Instead of wearing tennis shoes, he borrowed a pair of dress shoes from Pastor Lawrence. It was impossible to tell the shoes were a size too big for him.

Cindy was the perfect flower girl. She wore her faded floral sundress and a new pair of white sandals. Her hair was neatly braided, and she smiled all through the wedding and the reception.

We all tried to convince her to put down her flower basket after the wedding, but she refused. She carried it with her all afternoon and scattered yellow rose petals over the patio and half of the empty lot.

Mr. Martin surprised everyone. He wore a navy blue suit that smelled like mothballs, a white shirt and a striped tie. He still wore his old shoes, but he left his old felt hat at home.

He wasn't Irene's father, but no one would have ever known it. When he walked with her from the bookcases to the pastor at the front of the store, he grinned from ear to ear. Instead of standing with Grandma and Aunt Maude during the ceremony, he insisted on standing next to the groom.

As maid of honor, I wore my yellow sundress and white sandals and carried one yellow rose instead of a bouquet. Sarah undid my ponytail and combed my hair over my shoulders. I felt silly with it hanging down, but she assured me the new hairdo made me look more grown-up.

It was the wedding Clyde and Irene wanted, and I was proud of Pastor Lawrence's effort to keep it casual. Instead of the white robe he usually wore to perform weddings, he wore navy blue slacks and a white long-sleeved shirt. As the officiant, he carried his well-worn, leather-covered Bible.

Poor Mr. Wilson came down with an extreme case of gout early that morning. Dr. Lawrence ordered him to stay home with his foot elevated until the redness and swelling went away. He wanted to go to the wedding anyway, but Clyde said he was in too much pain to be there.

"The wedding wasn't fancy," I said to myself. "Except for Mr. Wilson's gout, it was perfect for Clyde and Irene."

Just as Miss Carter had agreed, the newlyweds spent their first night at her new bed and breakfast without charge. It was the only honeymoon they would have, and I was glad I negotiated it for them.

I pulled out the chair next to me and put my feet up on the seat. My muscles still ached from my fall, and it was impossible to hide the bandages on my legs and arms.

"Hey, Shirley."

I looked up at the open gate in the patio fence. Jim stood just outside, looking at me.

"Hi, Jim."

"I was driving up the alley and saw you sitting here by yourself," he said. "Glad to see you put your hair in a ponytail again."

"Thanks."

"What's going on?"

"I guess you could say I'm performing my community service."

"What?"

"It's just a little something between Miss Carter and me."

He walked over, pulled his baseball cap from his head and slapped it against his pant leg. Dried bits of chaff fell onto the clean patio.

"What are you talking about?"

"It's nothing."

He dragged a chair over to me, straddled the seat and crossed his arms on top of the backrest. His T-shirt and jeans were covered in dust.

"If it has to do with Miss Carter," he said, "it's definitely something."

I dropped my feet to the floor and sat up straight. When he looked me in the eye, I saw the concern on his face.

"Well?" he said. "Spill it."

"I told her I would clean up this place before I leave for home today, that's all."

"That's not all," he said, "and you know it."

275

I shifted a little in the chair, but no position was comfortable. When he continued to look at me, it was impossible for me not to tell him everything.

"If I agreed to clean up after the reception, she'd let me hold it here on the patio and the empty lot."

"And?"

"She'd let me pick Grandma's roses for the wedding."

"And?"

"Clyde and Irene could spend their first night together at the bed and breakfast for free."

"What else?"

"That's all," I said, "except for the two red roses for the cemetery."

He put his hat back on, stood up and shoved the chair back under the table. Without another word, he climbed the steps to the French doors and went inside the café.

I didn't have to wait long until he came back outside. He closed the doors, stomped down the steps and stood in front of me.

"How long have you been cleaning up out here?" he said. "Did you even get any breakfast?"

"I haven't been here that long, and I can eat on the train."

He took me by the hand and pulled me up from the chair. I forced my stiff body to stand up straight, and he wrapped his arms around me.

"Don't ever hide something like this from me again," he whispered in my ear. "We're in this together."

Before I could say anything, I heard crunching gravel and the rumble of truck engines coming up the alley. Jim let go of me, and we turned around to look out through the gate.

A line of trucks came to a stop along the edge of the empty lot, and boys of all ages poured out of the cabs. Each of them grabbed a rake or a mop or a bucket from the back of their trucks. Some even grabbed gunny sacks.

My mouth dropped open at the sight of them, and tears of relief ran down my cheeks. Seeing them walk toward us with all the tools made me feel less overwhelmed by the cleaning I still had to do.

"What did you do, Jim?"

"I used the café's phone to call a few friends for help, that's all."

Forty-six

Even with all the boys' help, it took longer to finish the cleanup than I expected. Taking time to stop at the cemetery to say goodbye to Dad and Grandpa was risky. The train back to South Bend wouldn't stop if we weren't there in time to raise the flag.

"You have ten minutes, young lady," Grandma said. "Jim and I will wait in the truck for you."

"Okay."

Jim pulled his father's truck to a stop parallel to the locked cemetery gate and jumped out of the cab. I moved George from my lap to Grandma's, picked up the red roses from the dashboard and jumped out right behind Jim.

"I'll say hello for you, too, Grandma."

I didn't wait for her reply. I clutched the roses to my chest, sidestepped behind the overgrown juniper bushes and found the break in the wrought-iron fence. I squeezed through the narrow opening and ran up the gravel service road.

When I got to the gazebo at the top of the hill, I stopped to catch my breath. Dad's and Grandpa's headstones stood in the bright sunlight only a few feet away. It was hard to believe a year had gone by since I had seen them.

The grass was neatly trimmed around the bases of the stones, but it was brown and brittle from the August heat. When I walked across it, it crackled under my sandals.

"Hi," I said. "I'm sorry I can't stay long this time."

I laid a rose on the base of both headstones and read the inscription on each one. After three years, Grandpa's stone was still shiny and easy to read, but not Dad's. The lettering on his was worn, and the stone was dull from seventeen years of harsh weather.

"I'm a senior in high school now," I said to them. "I probably won't be able to get here next summer to visit with you."

I heard one long blast from the horn in Mr. Spencer's truck, and I knew it was time to go. I reached out and touched the two stones. They looked cold and impersonal, but in my heart I knew Dad and Grandpa were looking down and listening to me.

"Grandma says hello, too," I said. "We love you both and miss you very much."

There was another long blast of the horn. I looked at the stones and the roses one last time and turned around. Without looking back, I ran down the service road to the wrought-iron fence and squeezed back through the small opening.

When I got to the truck, Jim was standing beside the driver's door, holding it open for me. I walked past him without a word and climbed into the cab.

"Are you alright, dear?"

"I'm okay, Grandma," I said. "I'm just sorry there wasn't time for you to go with me."

"I know you are," she said, "but we'll come together the next time you're in Willowdale."

I didn't know when that would be. Once I graduated high school and started college, there might not be another chance to visit Willowdale for a long time.

I settled on the seat again, and Grandma nudged George awake. He stood up, moved over to me and plopped down on my lap. When I leaned over and hugged him, he lifted his head and gave my nose a sloppy kiss.

"I'm really glad Aunt Maude let you come with us today, big guy."

Jim climbed into the truck, slammed the door closed and started the engine. He pulled a quick U-turn in the middle of Cemetery Road and pointed the truck toward the county road.

"Hang on," he said.

The flag stop wasn't far from the cemetery, but he pushed the accelerator nearly to the floor. The truck bounced over the pot holes in the gravel road and raised a rooster tail of dust behind us.

Grandma clutched the passenger armrest with one hand and braced her other hand against the dashboard. I wrapped my arms around George and wedged my knees against the dash to keep from sliding off the seat.

"Ye gods and little fishes," Grandma said. "Must we go so fast?"

Jim set his jaw and didn't ease his foot off the gas pedal until we arrived at the flag stop. He slowed the truck, pulled onto the grass next to the wooden platform and turned off the engine.

"We made it," he said.

In the distance, I heard the high-pitched whistle of the northbound train. Thanks to his crazy driving, we got there in time to signal the engineer.

Forty-seven

Jim jumped from the truck, ran to the open-sided shelter and yanked on a short rope hanging from a post. A wooden signal arm with a red flag on its end popped up.

While he secured the rope to a cleat, Grandma threw open the passenger door. We stepped out of the cab and inspected my suitcases in the truck bed. Both had tumbled all the way to the back and were covered in a layer of dust.

"At least they didn't bounce out," I said.

Jim ran back to the truck and stood next to me. He took off his baseball cap and ran his fingers through his hair.

"Sorry about your suitcases."

"Don't worry," I said. "I'll clean them up later."

He lifted them out of the truck, set them on the grass and slapped his cap against them. When that didn't dislodge much dust, he put his cap back on and carried them to the platform.

I reached inside the cab and snatched my purse off the floor. George was sprawled across the seat, sound asleep. I didn't want to wake him, so I gave him a gentle kiss on his wrinkled head and whispered in his ear.

"Goodbye, big guy."

I eased the passenger door closed. Grandma hooked her arm around my elbow, and we walked to the shelter together.

"Are you certain you packed all of your things?" she said.

"I think so."

The canvas suitcase was bulging with my clothes, the pennants Jim gave me and the letters I wrote to my dad. The overnight case was full of toiletries and a bagful of Aunt Maude's cookies.

My wallet was in the main compartment of my purse. There was just enough money in it to buy my ticket and a sandwich on the train. My savings account book was safely zipped in one of the side pockets.

"Before the train arrives," Grandma said, "there are two things that need to be discussed."

She walked over to a narrow wooden bench at the back of the shelter and sat down. Jim and I followed along and stood in front of her.

"I never told you, Shirley, how I planned to reimburse Jimmy for remodeling my old café."

"No, you never did," I said. "He told me it was just between the two of you."

"It was," she said. "Today, I'm fulfilling my half of our agreement."

"That really isn't necessary, Mrs. Ivey."

"Young man," she said. "We had an agreement, and I always honor my agreements."

"Yes, ma'am."

Jim and I sat down on either side of her, and she reached into a patch pocket on the front of her sundress. She pulled out a vehicle title, a registration slip and a leather cord. A key hung from the end of it.

"What are you doing, Grandma?"

"I didn't have the necessary funds to pay cash," she said. "We agreed he would get Robert's truck in exchange for all the materials he used."

"But, Grandma—"

"Mrs. Ivey," Jim said. "I don't feel right about taking the truck."

"Nonsense," she said. "It's a fair exchange, and it's exactly what my Robert would have done in my place."

"It's way too generous."

"Once your father begins his handyman job," she said, "you'll need transportation for school and your internship."

"Yes, but—"

I looked at him, and my eyes filled with tears. I loved Grandpa's truck. Even though Grandma couldn't drive, I didn't want her to give it away.

"There is one stipulation," she said. "I expect a ride, now and then, when the mood strikes me."

"Anytime you want," he said.

He took the papers and slipped them inside his back pants pocket. Then, he took the cord, hung it around his neck and put an arm around Grandma's shoulders.

"I'll take extra special care of Mr. Ivey's truck," he said. "I won't let you down."

"You never have, Jimmy."

When he finally took his arm from her shoulders, Grandma reached into the other patch pocket. She pulled out a small envelope and held it in both hands.

"The second thing we must discuss concerns you, Shirley."

"Me?"

"When I sold the café and the farmhouse," she said. "I knew how disappointed you were."

I turned toward her and looked into her eyes. She was the wisest person I knew, and it looked as though she had something serious on her mind.

"You didn't have a choice, Grandma," I said. "I did everything I could to help both of us get through it, that's all."

"You did that and more," she said. "I will always be grateful to you for spending these past two summers with me and giving me such joy."

I didn't want to cry, but I couldn't stop the tears. I unsnapped the clasp on my purse and found my hankie. After I wiped the tears from my face, I blew my nose and put the hankie in the pocket of my dress.

The train whistled again, and I saw the engine approaching from the south. There wasn't enough time left to properly say goodbye to two of the most important people in my life.

"Here, dear," Grandma said and slipped the small envelope inside my purse. "It's a little something I want you to have."

"What is it, Grandma?"

"You may look at it once you're on the train."

I snapped my purse closed, took Grandma's elbow in my hand and helped her stand up. While the three of us walked to the front of the platform, Jim picked up my bags and set them closer to the edge.

As the train drew closer and slowed to a crawl, he reached over and took my hand. I gave it a squeeze and looked up at him.

"Don't forget to write and tell me all about your job."

"How could I forget," he said with a big, toothy smile. "You won't let me."

When the train pulled to a stop, the conductor opened the door and jumped onto the platform. He pulled a small stool from inside the train, placed it under the door and held his hand out to me.

"Hurry," he said. "We only stop for a minute."

I dropped Jim's hand, threw my arms around his neck and gave him a huge hug. Then, I turned to Grandma and gave her a hug. When she put her arms around me and hugged me, too, I didn't want to let go.

"I love you, Grandma."

"Miss," the conductor said. "The train is leaving."

He picked up my bags and threw them onto the train, and I finally let go of Grandma. I took his hand, stepped onto the stool and climbed into the vestibule between the two coaches.

While I carried my bags into the front coach, the conductor picked up the stool, climbed aboard and slammed the door closed. The train lurched forward, and I found two empty seats at the center of the car.

I stacked my suitcase and overnight bag on the aisle seat and sat on the seat next to the window. When I looked outside, Jim and Grandma were on the platform waving at me.

After a few seconds, the train lurched again and picked up speed. I pressed my face to the glass and waved back at them until they were out of sight. There was nothing to do then but sit back and watch the countryside roll by.

"Ticket, Miss?"

I dug inside my purse for my wallet, counted out the correct fare and handed it to the conductor. He punched a hole in a ticket stub and slipped the stub into a pin on the overhead luggage rack. He tipped his hat at me, staggered up the aisle with the sway of the train and walked through the vestibule door.

When I put my wallet away, I saw the envelope Grandma gave me. I looked around to make sure no one was watching, took it out of my purse and opened it.

Inside was a savings book that looked identical to mine. I took it out of the envelope and thumbed through the pages. When I found the one with the balance of the account listed, my mouth dropped open.

"What is this, Grandma?" I said under my breath.

Behind the last page was a note tucked against the binding. I pulled it out, unfolded it and read what she wrote.

> Dear Shirley,
> You worked hard these past two summers, and I am very proud of you. I wanted you to learn the value of a dollar, and you did. You saved every paycheck to help with your college expenses.

I stopped reading for a moment and looked outside. Farmland rushed past the window, but inside the train, time seemed to stand still. I looked at the note again.

As a young woman, I dreamed of going to college and becoming a doctor. In those days, I had neither the money nor the opportunity to realize my dream.

When you began saving your paychecks, I created a separate account of my own. Every time you deposited a dollar into your savings account, I deposited two dollars into mine.

"I don't understand, Grandma," I whispered. "Why did you give me your book?"

My dream of becoming a doctor has come and gone, but your dream of becoming a teacher has just begun. With both of our accounts, you should have enough money for your first two years of college tuition and books.

I only ask two things of you in return. Do your very best in school and continue to follow your dream.

Love, Grandma

I refolded the note and tucked it back inside the book. I leaned against the seat back, closed my eyes and listened to the rhythmic clicks of the train wheels against the track.

Holding the little book over my heart, I pictured Grandma on the platform waving goodbye. Her faith in me and my dream was the greatest gift I had ever received.

"I promise not to let either of us down, Grandma," I said out loud, "and I always keep my promises."

About the Author

Carla J. Underwood was born in Indiana and grew up in the northwest corner of the state. She learned the challenges and the rewards of living in a small community.

She embraced those small-town ideals and opted for a small, out-of-state university. She earned a B.A. degree in Speech Pathology and Audiology.

She and her husband now live in a small town in the desert Southwest. They share their home with their twelve-year-old pug.

More about the Willowdale, Indiana stories– *Mrs. Ivey's Café*, *A Dog's Life* and *A Granddaughter's Promise* –is found at www.mudpiespress.com.

www.ingramcontent.com/pod-product-compliance
Lightning Source LLC
Chambersburg PA
CBHW050712180626
46814CB00002B/406